Dobbie —

Enjoy The Story!

Support The Search
for a Cure!

In Jesus

Burl

By the Hand of His Grace

D.H. BARBARA

People, places and events in this novel are fictional and although some may bear resemblance to people you may know...isn't that the point? Lakeville and its residents exist totally and exclusively in my own head, and on these pages.

Visit D.H. Barbara online at
www.dhbarbara.com

Social Media:
Twitter: @dhbarbara1
Facebook: facebook.com/DHBarbara
Goodreads: goodreads.com/DHBarbara

For every dear one who has been in the
battle

For every person who has struggled as they
watched a loved one endure

For every health care professional who tends
these special patients

For every person who has been touched by
breast cancer; spouse, child, parent,
extended family and friend

Keep on fighting; keep on believing; keep on
loving

Psalm 91

He who dwells in the shelter of the Most High will abide in the shadow of the Almighty.

I will say to the LORD, "My refuge and my fortress, my God, in whom I trust."

For he will deliver you from the snare of the fowler and from the deadly pestilence.

He will cover you with his pinions, and under his wings you will find refuge; his faithfulness is a shield and buckler.

You will not fear the terror of the night, nor the arrow that flies by day, nor the pestilence that stalks in darkness, nor the destruction that wastes at noonday.

A thousand may fall at your side, ten thousand at your right hand, but it will not come near you.

You will only look with your eyes and see the recompense of the wicked.

Because you have made the LORD your dwelling place—the Most High, who is my refuge—no evil shall be allowed to befall you, no plague come near your tent.

For he will command his angels concerning you to guard you in all your ways.

On their hands they will bear you up, lest you strike your foot against a stone.

You will tread on the lion and the adder; the young lion and the serpent you will trample underfoot.

"Because he holds fast to me in love, I will deliver him; I will protect him, because he knows my name.

When he calls to me, I will answer him; I will be with him in trouble; I will rescue him and honor him.

With long life I will satisfy him and show him my salvation."

Contents

Section One: Azure

Section Two: Indigo

Section Three: Midnight

Section Four: A Hint of Cerulean

Azure

Amid the forested corner of southeastern Pennsylvania, the small town of Lakeville was nestled. Its quiet core streets, populated with post-WWII housing gave way to a more sprawling outskirts. Children biked to school and played in the streets, staying out until the sun went down during the summer months. The town possessed the beauty and intimacy of days gone by while its residents plunged headlong into the 21st century.

On a side street, the warm spring sunshine streamed through the freshly washed windows at Autumn Young Pyoriasaari's modest home. Her spring cleaning over with, Autumn admired the results. Wood floors sparkled, carpets smelled fresh, couch cushions were fluffed and inviting. She pulled polka-dotted rubber gloves from her hands with relish, dropped them in the sink and vigorously washed her hands. The anticipation of being completely spoiled with a manicure and pedicure, another annual, though much more enjoyable, event brought a smile to her face.

"I know what that smile is all about," her husband's voice reached her before his arms encircled her waist. "That's the 'I deserve this!' grin." He kissed her cheek, squeezed lightly, and then released her to dry her hands. He kissed her cheek, squeezed lightly, and then released her to dry her hands. Paul walked across the kitchen to the calendar hanging on the wall next to the house phone. The date was circled with a bright green marker line and one of their daughters had written 'Yay!' in pink across the box.

"The girls are excited too, I see," he mused, a throaty laugh following. Paul Pyoriasaari caught more than Autumn's eye the first time she heard that distinctive laugh. It didn't seem so long ago…was it possible almost twenty years had passed?

He was new to their congregation and almost finished with his degree. At the annual church picnic following the Memorial Day parade, Autumn rounded up the children to play a game of *Mother, May I?* When she lifted her gaze from the child asking permission to take four giant steps, she found Paul in conversation with her father, laughing over something said between them. Any man who braved her father's company, whose rough and tumble past was no secret among the congregation, deserved her admiration.

"Yes, they are. Their focus is more on the allowance they get to spend at the craft store, but they enjoy getting their nails painted, too." Autumn replaced the hand towel on a hook. She glanced out of the greenhouse window, to her garden. "Shoots are starting to come up."

"I'm certain we'll have a bumper crop this year. You spent enough time and energy giving that patch a thorough turning over and fertilizing." He picked up a battered attaché case. "I'm going to collect some papers and run, Belle. Enjoy your day being pampered.

They met in the center of the kitchen for a parting embrace before going their separate ways; he, to his office and she, to the stairs leading to the master bathroom.

The Chester County mall was only a half hour drive by the highway that sat on the town's western border. Enjoying the fine art of window shopping, Autumn strolled down the cobblestone alongside her mother, Samantha Young Revell. They kept a watchful eye on Autumn's two daughters walking ahead; they had stopped to giggle at a window display in a baby clothing boutique.

"I miss the fabric store in town, but it's fun to get out to the mall," Autumn said. "But, it makes me feel a little behind the times regarding fashion. Just look at that!" She pointed to the mannequins inhabiting a sleek store-front, popular with the 20-something crowd. "I don't think I would have worn that in high school!"

"No, that was much more your sister's style. Sunnie excelled at employing shock value." Sammie nibbled at the giant, butter laden pretzel in her hand. "I don't think I have enough napkins." She licked at a gob dripping down her finger.

Autumn handed her a spare. "When do Rob, Aina and River come back?"

Sammie's smile grew. "Tonight! I miss them. This is the first time they've gone away without me. Unavoidable, and it was a nice change. But, it's time for them to be home." She recalled some highlights of times the family visited her sister-in-law in Virginia. She was certain her husband and two youngest would come home well fed and exhausted from the mandatory Southern rites of visitation.

The girls were waiting at the entrance to the large fabric shop as Autumn and Sammie caught up to them. Jacquie, the elder, smiled at her freshly manicured hands a moment, then turned with anticipation. "Can we look at the cross stitch supplies with Gramma while you shop?"

Autumn glanced back to her mother, who nodded her agreement of the proposed plan. "Nothing complicated. Emmie is just starting out. Stay within your budget."

The girls agreed before pulling their grandmother into the store, eagerly chattering about their latest crafting projects. Autumn followed, a whisper of thanksgiving on her lips for the close relationship her mother and daughters enjoyed. She'd had no such thing growing up. One set of grandparents had been unknown and her maternal grandmother had been far from a warm and welcoming person.

Eleanor Slessor left nothing to the imagination. She was a distant and hard woman, vocal in the extreme in her dislike of her son-in-law. The discord kept them from more than perfunctory visiting, even after his death.

Her late father spoke little of his mother, or any family. Autumn and her other sister, Storm, would sometimes speculate about Grandmother Young what she may have looked like, or if she would have taught them how to make cookies. The paternal relatives were always surrounded by a shroud of mystery.

Pulling herself from the odd assortment of memories that had sprung up, Autumn walked towards the displayed row of bright calicos. "The kitchen needs a pick me up. Curtains, placemats and napkins?" she pondered to herself while getting lost in yards of cotton, rolls of bias tape, spools of thread and the latest fashion patterns.

"Can we stop by Uncle Si's?" Emily implored from the back seat. Autumn, peeked at her in the rear view mirror. If she had parental approval, Emily's diet would consist exclusively of meals from her uncle's coffee shop and her father's easy Sunday dinners, Autumn's own fine cooking notwithstanding. She always gushed over baked Parmesean chicken and herbed rice as well as curly spaghetti with meatballs. Emily, Autumn was certain, would grow to become a food journalist.

"He's closed now, sweetie. We'll stop in tomorrow, it's a nice treat on Saturday mornings. Maybe your father can join us before he goes to the clinic."

"That would be fun!" Jacquie chimed in, brushing a strand of deep golden brown hair from her eyes. "We haven't done that in a long time!"

"I think we will. We can walk to the library afterward." Autumn flipped the blinker to turn off the highway. As they drove past the Lakeville Country Club, she honked and called to the girls, "Quick, wave! There's John Anthony and Colin!"

They waved, catching a glimpse of their cousins who lived deep back in the wooded area opposite the golf course. Autumn waved to Sunnie, her oldest sister and mother of the boys, who was gathering mail from a large security box at the entrance to the secluded property.

The road curved into Lakeville proper. More houses appeared, becoming closer together as they neared the center of town. Businesses began to dot the landscape, including the more modern chiropractic office of her husband. She noted his car parked in his designated spot and smiled. Barring any emergency visits, he would be home early this evening.

Autumn navigated through the narrow streets to their pleasant Cape Cod house. Flower beds, exploding with multi-colored foxglove, yarrow and wild roses highlighted the windows on either side of the entry. She noticed the door was beginning to show some wear, and made a note to plan for its repainting before fall.

Punched metal ornamentation on the chimenera cast shadows on the patio that night after the girls were in bed. Relaxing, glass of wine in hand, Autumn leaned back on the lounge chair next to Paul. The hum of the dishwasher through the open screen door provided background music as they gazed up at the stars blanketing Lakeville.

"I like this one. What's it called?" She took another small taste. Sweet tones of peach and a warming touch of cinnamon burst forth.

"It's a peach Reisling from a vineyard in upstate New York. I added a cinnamon stick, at Silas's suggestion, when I opened it a few weeks ago. Nice touch, I must say." He enjoyed a swig of his own.

"The girls were disappointed you couldn't have breakfast with us tomorrow."

He chuckled, placing the glass on a small table alongside the double wide lounger. "Oh, I'm not sure Emmie is so fussed over it. After all, she gets to have biscotti and fancy coffee."

"You'll more than make up for it on Sunday. We should start saving for her food-oriented career now. Si's school is not at all on the 'affordable' option list."

He took her hand, caressing the back with his thumb. "They'll be fine, Belle. We already have a good base on their college or wedding savings. My parents pay into their accounts every holiday. Don't fret about the future."

She pushed against him playfully. "What? I can't plan ahead?"

He turned to her, his eyes expressive in the firelight. "The only plans I want you making right now are for when this glass of wine is finished."

She laughed. "That's easy. Wash the glasses, then go finish cutting out that fabric…"

"You think so?" He pulled her closer, whispering his own alternative plans in her ear, which she readily agreed were far better.

Wynter Delights customers overflowed out of the door and onto Maple Street. Silas's coffee shop in the heart of Lakeville offered three café tables on the sidewalk in front of the large window, which were taken up by customers soaking in the early morning sun as they enjoyed their coffee and pastry. Autumn and the girls excused themselves as they cut through the queue to enter the shop. Emily and Jacquie hurried to the two freshly abandoned stools at the counter.

Greetings sounded from behind the counter when Silas burst from the kitchen, a tray of biscotti fresh from the ovens on his shoulder. He slid it into the display case, scooped two from the end and placed them in front of his nieces before moving to the register beside his wife. "I can help you," he called to the next person in line.

Autumn waited for the crowd to diminish to make them all cups of hot coffee. She first brought some for the girls, along with packets of flavored creamers, before going back to make her own. The pace of the shop slowed, eventually emptying of satisfied weekenders off on their adventures and errands. Wynter bounded over as soon as she could move away from the register, greeting the family with her large and friendly smile and tight, loving hugs.

"Good to see you! What are you doing today?" She paid close attention to Jacquie's run down of their itinerary, and gushed over Emily's first cross stitch project, a small purple rose. Silas, apron covered in various ingredients of the morning, left the kitchen long enough to hug his sister and comment on his wife's never-ending energy and enthusiasm in the midst of the usual Saturday morning rush.

The remainder of the morning was spent walking to the library and back home. After the lunch dishes were cleared and dinner was simmering on the stove, Autumn entered her cheerful sewing and craft room. To the hum of the serger she prayed over her family, church and town. Her curtains were completed with offerings of thanksgiving for the closeness of her large family.

Autumn would long remember the beauty of that Sunday afternoon as the last before her existence was forever changed. It was soon to be refashioned with an ease in which she could transform a bolt of plain black cotton blend into a knock-out cocktail dress.

A deep assurance of her faith lifted in her heart, as if on the currents of late April warmth, up into the deeply hued sky. She greeted the reverend after the service, returning his hearty handshake. When Paul stepped forward to compliment the morning's message, Autumn walked over to her sister-in-law Julie and her energetic young boys.

"Jude did wonderfully today," she said, reaching to ruffle one nephew's hair. "His first solo! I'm so impressed. He's only been with the choir a few months."

"Rev Bell has had this plan for years," Julie said, pride for her husband beaming in her countenance. Not one member of the Young clan was surprised that Jude finally filled his mother's vacated seat in the Madison Avenue Baptist Church choir. "He said he's been praying for your brother to join ever since he was a teenager."

Other pleasantries and family tidings were exchanged before Autumn bid them goodbye. With Paul's hand in hers, they walked to their car, stopping here and there to chat with friends along the way.

Once home, she set out to her other happy spot, the garden, to rid it of the weeds that would make every attempt to choke the life from her tomato vines. Content with the blessings surrounding her, she knelt in the loam and pulled on well-worn gardening gloves. She breathed deeply of the rich scents wafting through the neighborhood; heady florals and pine, the first backyard cookouts of the season. A perfect Sunday afternoon.

The sermon replayed in her mind as she worked, yanking the offending shoots from the base of the tender, young plants. "*We must live fully and completely for our Living Lord,*" Reverend Bell's passionate challenge issued. "*Will we, as our final hymn states, take and offer all to Him, for His glory?*"

"Thank you so much, Lord," she breathed, tears brimming her lashes, "You've given me so much. All I can say is thank you and give it all back to you."

Autumn moved down one row and returned to her task, humming the final hymn sung before Reverend Bell's benediction. The congregational singing that morning had been especially spirited. She heard her brother's clear and melodic baritone as she crooned the words.

Take my life and let it be…

Chapter 2

Paul observed his wife working in her beloved garden from the window above his desk. Beauty that had stolen his heart years before shone bright as the sun. In every sense, Autumn was a woman as the Bible described in the last chapter of Proverbs. She nurtured their daughters, kept careful watch over the household, and was beautiful to the depths of her heart. He felt he was a blessed man.

"Daddy? Are we having supper soon?"

He turned from the lovely outdoor view to his younger daughter. Her bright and inquisitive eyes looked to him, and a gap-toothed smile shone. *Yes Lord*, he thought, *I am extremely blessed.*

He tousled her hair, light in shade as his and as wavy as her mother's. "Of course, sweetness. The usual?"

"Oh, yes!" She skipped to the kitchen, informing her sister of the choice with delight. "Jax! We're having breakfast for supper!"

He followed in her wake, amused by her excitement over a simple frittata. He pulled a large frying pan from the cabinet beside the stove, placing it atop the burner. He assembled the necessary elements for their standard Sunday evening meal, dubbed "scrambled sausage eggs" by Emily when she was a toddler.

When Autumn later walked into the house, she was enveloped in the homey aroma of spicy pork frying in an obscene portion of butter. As Paul whisked near a dozen eggs together with a concoction of his own ingredients in a bright orange bowl, he flashed a grin that released butterflies in the chambers of her heart.

"Scrambled sausage eggs?" She pulled the floppy sunhat off and hung it on a peg by the sliding glass door.

"Of course, it's Sunday. What else?" He poured the mixture into the pan. A mouthwatering sizzle filled the kitchen. "I told Emmie she could help me turn it over. She's been waiting for her turn."

"I'll set the table as soon as I wash up," Autumn offered as she crossed to the sink, pushing the faucet with her elbow.

"No need, Jacquie took care of it. What you can do is pick out a bottle of wine to accompany the sunset later." His smile meaningfully deepened before he turned back to check the progress of the frittata.

"In that case," she leaned towards him and whispered. "I'll run upstairs and grab a quick shower." Their eyes met, and they shared a quick kiss. "I say we finish the peach Reisling," she added before placing the dampened paper towel in the trash bin.

"Excellent choice. Don't be long," he called, his attention taken by her graceful gait as she left the room. A tap on his arm brought him back to the kitchen, his small assistant chef and dinner at hand.

The bedside lamp set ablaze quelled the building romantic atmosphere. "Paul, what on earth..."

"Shh, please do as I say. Put your arm behind your head, yes..."

Autumn shaded her eyes, unsettled by her husband's suddenly clinical attitude. Their marriage bed became an examination table as he delicately pressed and probed firm breast tissue. Years of assisting him in the office enabled Autumn to read the subtle change of expression to one of concern. Her mouth went dry when his trained, sensitive fingers reached the object of suspicion.

"What is it?"

Her whisper lingered between them a moment. When he applied pressure, she winced with discomfort. A frown marred his handsome face, the tell-tale mark of a doctor about to pronounce an unwanted diagnosis.

"You have a lump; it's small," he amended at the flash of fear in her eyes. "I'd say the size of a pea...perhaps a bit larger."

"Impossible," she insisted. She sat upright, cupping the rebellious flesh. "I do an exam of my own every month. Nothing was there."

He rose, pulling his robe from the foot rail on his way to the dresser. "I know it wasn't, but it is now. I'm going to call my father."

That announcement cut short her re-examination of the area. She left the bed and caught him before he started dialing the number.

"I'd prefer to call my doctor, rather than alarm him."

The first time he got lost in her deep brown eyes, they were clear and beautiful and full of the same sentiment he felt. They were now clouded by trepidation. He masked his own concern, forcing a slight smile to appear.

"You know I would not impose on him if it wasn't important. No matter our differences in practice, I'd like his opinion. After all, he's one of the top breast surgeons in Philadelphia. Make us some tea while I call, please?"

The very fact that Paul wanted his father's opinion shot a cold dart of fear into Autumn's chest. He had sorely disappointed the man with his choice of medical venue. Dr. Paul Pyoriasaari, Sr. never set foot inside his son's chiropractic clinic, nor congratulated him upon the success he enjoyed in the field.

Phone in hand, he kissed her temple before leaving her to put on night clothes. She prayed as she dressed, running her fingers over the area one more time. The lump had not evaporated; knowing it was not a figment of their imagination made it seem larger

The muted light of the kitchen cast a golden hue over the familiar objects on the countertops. Paul was seated at the table, deep in discussion by the time she entered. She moved about quietly, turning on the kettle, taking down their favored mugs. Her hands trembled when she placed tea bags into them. The conversation took a turn into rapid Finnish, then exploded back to English.

"Yes, Father, I know! I'm not taking it lightly; would I have called you? I'll speak to Autumn about it and get back to you...Yes, tomorrow...Fine, fine...hello to mother. I'll talk to you tomorrow. Thank you, Father... Yes...Goodbye." When he set the phone beside the cup Autumn placed in front of him, Paul took on the exhausted look associated with completing a marathon.

"I suppose he wants me there first thing in the morning?" She sat next to him, waiting to hear the verdict. Paul stirred a dollop of honey into his tea and pondered the conversation a moment before releasing a deep breath.

"Of course, it was his immediate reaction." He pushed the small stoneware pot back to the center of the table. "Frankly, I'm certain his first thought was that I'd let this go too long and all hope is lost. I assured him you are diligent with your monthly exams, and that we don't solely rely on my 'speculative, natural healing methods' all of the time."

She clasped his hand. "It's his area of specialty. He's seen the very best and absolute worst cases. This may only be a clogged duct or something...not very serious."

"Em is almost eight—it's been a while since you nursed an infant. Yet, it could be," he backpedalled. "It's likely not, though. Call your doctor in the morning; let's take it one step at a time."

They held hands, finishing their drinks in silence. Disturbing scenarios raced through their minds. Neither was willing, for the moment, to share the fears and concerns which began cropping up. Before long, Paul cleared his throat.

"He wants us to come next weekend; he works with another surgeon who will agree to see you then." Paul knew every objection she would voice, and they came as rapidly as he suspected.

"Paul, that's a dinner with my family. We never miss it. I don't expect a doctor I have never met to rearrange their schedules to indulge his…"

He held up a hand. "Your family will understand. This is important."

Rumpled blonde hair and Nordic good looks did not soften the blow of his insistent tone. She'd heard it time and time again at the office when a stubborn client would not participate in their healing regimen. No argument against his decision would be heard. Autumn placed her cup down decisively.

"I'll talk to Mom tomorrow. The girls will be thrilled with a few days in Philly; maybe we can squeeze in a trip to the zoo, too." Hooking an arm through his, she nestled against his shoulder. "We'll get through it. I'm sure it's nothing."

He breathed in the scent of her hair, relishing the warmth of her touch. These small, inconsequential things suddenly seemed vital to existence. "Come back to bed with me," he requested, his tone deep and husky.

Eager to erase the concern in both of their minds, she smiled before rising from the table. They walked back up the stairs hand in hand, leaving the worry over the uninvited guest in their lives at the table for the remainder of the night.

The girls were settled into their school routines and Autumn had scrubbed the main level bathroom within military sanitation standards before she gathered up her nerve to call the doctor. She sat at the desk in Paul's office and dialed, each beep made by the buttons she pushed revealing new concerns.

"Doctor Swirsky's office, please hold a moment."

Great, she thought, scanning the desk for anything to distract her apprehensive thoughts and pass the time. She grabbed at a pile of colored index cards. Scripture verses, written in Paul's neat hand, met her momentary need. She read through four cards, and was beginning the fifth, before the receptionist returned.

"I'm sorry for the delay. How may I direct your call?"

"This is Autumn Pyoriasaari. I need to see Dr Swirsky as soon as possible, please."

"Can you spell your last name?"

Of course I can. She shook off irritability and attempted to be pleasant. "P-Y-O..."

"Yes, I have you. May I call you Autumn?" Upon agreement, she continued with a list of scripted responses. "Has your address changed since your last visit? Phone number? Is this for a routine examination?"

"No!" Hysteria was brimming. "No. Is it possible to speak with Dr. Swirsky?

Disdain oozed through the receiver. "He's quite busy, Autumn. Can you hold another moment?"

"Do I have a choice?" She shook her head, then offered an apology. "Excuse me, please, I'm a bit frazzled. I'd be happy to hold."

Muzak filled her ear with no warning. Berating herself for displaying snappishness, she continued to read through the pile of cards, quickly picking up the color sequence Paul established. The green cards were verses that spoke of peace. Yellow was for worship. Blue, praise. Autumn placed the pile down when Dr. Swirsky came on the line.

"Hello, Mrs. P. How are you?"

She laughed, a release to the anxiety that had built. The doctor made no attempts, ever, at pronouncing her married name in all the years she had been a patient. "I'm fine...well, no, I'm not. I need to come see you. We...I...well, Paul discovered a lump in my right breast."

"I see. Have you been in pain?" She replied in the negative. The doctor said something unintelligible, then asked, "How long have you had it?"

"I'm not sure. I didn't feel it during my last cycle. I check every month." She folded a blank card as many times as she possibly could.

"Can you describe it to me now?"

Although Autumn had examined the lump many times since it's discovery, she found an audible, physical description difficult. Her hand massaged the offending area. "It's small. Paul said the size of a pea. I can't really tell. It's hard, almost like a marble. I didn't notice a visible difference in the breast or skin, and I've had no discharge."

More background chatter occurred before the doctor said, "Wednesday, between noon and two is open. What time best suits you?"

"I'll take twelve-thirty. Paul should be able to come, it's his lunch. Thank you so much."

"I'll see you then." A feeling of finality settled over her; the appointment was set. "Please, don't worry until we see what this is."

Easy for you, she screamed inside. When the call disconnected, she put the phone in the cradle, dropped her head to her hands and cried.

The clock in the waiting area read 2:37. Paul checked the scheduled visits, noting that Mrs. Jackson and her three children would be arriving at two forty-five. Three lovely, albeit very active, boys under the age of ten, which allotted a very small window of time to call home.

"Lucy, I'll be on the phone with Autumn. When the Jacksons arrive, knock twice, then plug in the Jonah vegetable movie for them. It seems to be their favorite.

"Very good, Doctor Paul." She reached into the bottom drawer and pulled out the requested video. As she set it on the desk, Paul was reminded of how thankful he was to have his wife's counsel in hiring Lucy. She had been in the women's shelter when Autumn implored him to give her a chance working for them. The successful stint was well into its seventh year, and Lucy was newly married.

Returning to his office, he snatched up the phone. Speed dial did not seem quite as fast as it normally was. He was greeted by a stifled sniffle. "It's me. Is everything all right?"

"I suppose. He'll see us on Wednesday. Can you extend your lunch?" More sniffles and a veiled attempt to blow her nose followed.

"Of course. Will we take the girls with us, or will your mother watch them?"

"I didn't think that far ahead, yet. I'll call mom, or Julie. I hate to have to explain the situation over and over again." Worry cracked her voice, followed by a sob.

"Stay calm, my Belle," he said, irritated he was stuck late in the office. "Dry those beautiful eyes. How's the garden?"

She laughed at his attempt to divert her wild imaginings. "I'll go out and see." She blew her nose once more. "I love you, Paul."

"And, I love you back." A light knock sounded. "I must run, the Jackson's are here. I'll be home at seven, and I expect to see dirty gardening gloves on the patio." He disconnected the call, taking a moment to capture his own thoughts before tackling his liveliest patients.

Chapter 3

When the phone in her mother's kitchen rang, Autumn's two youngest siblings raced into the room. They skidded to a stop when they saw their father claiming the prize at the end of their impromptu battle. One stern glance from him had them both seated at the table, hands folded, as they quietly awaited him to complete the call.

"No, Autumn," Rob answered his stepdaughter, "your mother is out. Is there something I can help with?" River swiped a kick at his sister's chair, earning him a warning tap on the shoulder. "I don't see why we can't. Unless your mother planned something I'm not aware of, we can watch them. I'll have her call you when she gets in."

When he disconnected the call, he turned first to his son. "Don't try to blame your sister for your troubles. You raced in here as though the house was on fire. You've both been told that is unacceptable."

"I know, but…" His excuse died before it had a chance to completely form. He was familiar with the behavior expected by his father. He sat up and turned toward the girl across the table. "I'm sorry, Aina. I shouldn't have kicked your chair."

She preened a bit before she caught her father's censuring gaze. "'sokay, Riv," she said, meekly lowering her eyes.

"Accepting an apology without gloating is an important lesson to learn." Rob allowed them time to ponder that deep truth before asking, "What were the two of you doing before you came barreling in here?"

"I was practicing demi pointe—Riv was watching something on the military channel." Aina's respectful answer was approved with a swift nod from her brother.

Rob's expression softened. The children he never dreamed he'd father were a constant source of delight, even when correction was called for. He sent a silent praise to heaven for the privilege and allowed them to go back to their previous activities.

When Sammie returned from her errands, she found her second family outside. Rob was tossing a ball with River while Aina performed impossible gymnastic feats on the play equipment. They called a greeting to her as she crossed the lawn.

He threw the ball back to River before sweeping her into a hug, both delighting and disgusting their children. They laughed and started walking towards the deck, Rob's arm draped across her shoulder.

"Autumn called while you were gone," he said. "She asked if you were free on Wednesday to watch the girls. I told her it wasn't a problem, but that you would call to confirm when you got in. She sounded upset."

Sammie glanced at him. "Autumn? Upset?" She pondered imagined reasons until they reached the steps. "I'll go call now. I'll be down in time for dinner."

"What are we having?" Rob asked, a hopeful tone to his query. He laughed when she called over her shoulder that whatever he chose to pull out of the freezer and put in the oven was fine with her.

Before heading to her bedroom Sammie emptied her bag of receipts, and placed her keys on a hook in the laundry room. Once she changed into a comfortable outfit and washed her hands, she picked up the phone. Autumn answered on the first ring.

"Hi, sweetie. Rob said you…" A rush of chatter from her daughter interrupted.

"I have a lump, Mom. Paul found it last night. The soonest Dr. Swirsky could see me is on Wednesday and Julie had something scheduled, and I hated to call you…" She paused to take a breath. "I'm scared. What if…"

"Autumn, honey, slow down! Where are the girls?" Sammie perched on the edge of the bed, anxious to hear what Autumn had to say.

"They're upstairs, reading. We had an early dinner since Paul works late tonight—but they know I'm upset about something."

"Okay, good." Sammie was relieved they weren't within earshot of their conversation. "Start over. Paul found a lump. A large one?"

"No. It's small. I think. I don't know." Autumn pressed her fingers against the spot. She recalled the discovery and subsequent phone conversations. "Doctor P. wants us to come next weekend. Of course, he has a friend who can see me right away."

"That's wonderful. A second opinion is helpful." Sammie twisted a handkerchief between her fingers and prayed silently. *Lord, no! Not cancer.*

"I'll see what Dr. Swirsky has to say first. I kept myself away from the computer today. I don't want to research it. I want this to be nothing, but Mom, what if it's not?" Anxiety ramped her voice up several octaves.

"It may be nothing. I know that it's the natural response, but don't let fear take control of you. Do you want to pray?"

The question—one her mother had asked a hundred times before, in almost as many circumstances—brought the tears Autumn had been forcing away. Sammie ached to be with her, to hold her close and assure her things would work out. "I can be right over," she offered.

"No, Mom. It's fine." Autumn wrestled some tissues from a box on the desk. "Paul will be home soon. I'm just a little worked up. I'll be fine. I would love for you to pray, I haven't been able to all afternoon." As much as she hated to admit that fact, it somehow cleared her mind. More tears flowed as she prayed silently along with Sammie. Cleansing and calming.

After a span of silence, Sammie spoke. "Why don't you bring the girls over tomorrow? We'll have dinner, then they can stay. You and Paul can have a night to yourselves to talk and pray." She paused. "Have you told anyone else?"

"Besides Julie, no. I'd rather not—until after we visit Philadelphia." Sammie heard the unspoken plea for privacy, unusual for their close family.

"I understand. Talk to Paul about tomorrow. Call me in the morning. We can reschedule the family dinner."

"I don't know. I hate to put everyone out. I'll talk to Paul about that. Thank you."

Sammie held the receiver in her hand after Autumn hung up, prayed again, then dialed a familiar number; one she called often. It was difficult, at best, to call on her oldest and dearest friend to include one of her own beloved daughters in the very private and exclusive club over which Victoria Reiger presided. When the call was answered, Sammie broke down and allowed the fears in her heart for her child to have their voice.

The hospital buzzed with morning routines; nurses and orderlies greeted the doctor as they passed him in the hallway. Dr. Paul Pyoriasaari, Sr. strolled through his domain with a practiced, benevolent expression in place. His tailored suit set off his stoic features and his impressive fitness level. Racquetball three times per week and a healthy diet kept him competitive with the younger doctors.

From his office on the third floor, the view overlooking Philadelphia was breathtaking. He often wondered, as he looked toward Independence Hall, if his ancestors walked past this spot. There had been a Pyoriasaari residing in the city since the wake of what was termed the Great Migration, a long and proud line of doctors. Until his son.

His customary mental deliberation of that subject was shoved aside in the current unease over his daughter-in-law. A beautiful girl, Dr. Pyoriasaari had always thought, similar in build and coloring to his own sister, kind and caring. The possibility of this insidious disease invading her body infuriated and concerned him.

He witnessed the destruction of the strongest marriages under the stress of medical treatment. Emotional torment which reduced self-assured women of high industry to timid creatures unable to speak up and be their own advocates.

He'd seen successes and triumphs over the course of his career, but the failures dogged him. The loss of hope reflected in the haunted eyes of loved ones, diagnosed in a terminal stage. Dr Pyoriasaari placed his hand on the frame of the panoramic window and closed his eyes against the images filed deep in the hippocampus. A formerly vibrant woman wasted to nothing, her grip on his hand weakening as she faded into eternity. His promise to her to fight against the disease when he earned his degree.

"This will not happen to her," he vowed to himself. "Paul must take a reasonable stand on this. He must listen to the experts. None of this playing with oils and vitamins. No, he'll see reason when it's his own wife's life at stake, and not a stranger." He turned from the magnificent view to his desk.

Organized from right to left, it was the picture of perfection. Not a speck of dust could be found on the surface. File folders were neatly stacked, ready for review; the pens in the holder were all facing the same direction. It belonged to a man who was always in control, confident that his conclusions were the correct ones.

On the wall, directly above his chair, surrounded by his many accolades and degrees, hung a family portrait. His son and granddaughters surrounded the loveseat on which he and his wife sat. There, beside Paul, stood Autumn, the very representation of happiness and health. He stood staring at it until a light knock forced his attention to the door.

"Good morning, Doctor." A young man walked in, a leather bound agenda in one hand and a cup of coffee in the other. "Are you ready to review your day?"

"Yes, Elliot. Thank you." He took the mug Elliot offered, inhaling the rich aroma before savoring the first sip. "I have a consult with Dr. Mahr at noon. That will take my afternoon, most likely. Before that?"

Elliot settled into a plush chair, and opened the calendar to the day's page. His recital of scheduled events droned. The doctor realized he was expected to answer a question when the room silenced.

"Excuse me, Elliot. My mind is elsewhere." He rounded the desk and sat. "There are no surgeries, correct?"

"Not today, sir." He maintained his composure, although his thorough report was ignored.

"That will be all for now. Please be certain to schedule an extra half hour for lunch in your day. I believe you mentioned you have a sister in town this week?" He held out his hand for the agenda.

Elliot brightened, sitting up a bit and straightening his tie. "Yes. I was hoping to take her to *le Sojour* for lunch." He passed the itinerary to the doctor. "She enjoys French cuisine. Thank you for remembering."

Dr Pyoriasaari laughed. "Ah, *Sojour*! Please mention my name if Chef Martinne insists she is booked." He skimmed the neat handwriting. "I have a light morning, I'm sure I can manage without you. Go and enjoy your time with her. I will hold you to task tomorrow." He dismissed Elliot with a nod.

The young man rose, thrilled yet concerned. "I appreciate that, Doctor, but are you quite…"

"Elliot, shall I dock your pay?" Dr Pyoriasaari looked sternly across the desk, placing the book on one corner.

"Of course not, sir."

"Don't…what is the expression? 'Stop looking gift donkeys in the mouth'?"

A good natured laugh erupted between them. "Yes doctor. Thank you. I'll see you in the morning, sir. I'll leave the agenda on my desk, in case you need it." He picked up the book on his way out of the office. Dr Pyoriasaari overheard his animated voice as he spoke to someone on the phone while wrapping up his work for the unscheduled free day. When he glanced over, he saw a mirror image of his own desk. Tidy, free of dust, the agenda placed in the exact middle of the landscape.

He swiveled the chair toward the picture window. He sipped the coffee, jotting questions on a pad in preparation to meet with his colleague.

Paul pulled off his glasses, massaging the bridge of his nose between his thumb and forefinger. Hours had passed since he arrived at the clinic and he'd been sequestered in front of a screen, researching treatment options to present to Autumn.

Not unwilling to go a traditional route, Paul's preferential treatment options were best suited to early detection. He'd hardly scratched the surface of the one hundred sixty-some-odd tabs he had opened in his browser when his cell phone startled him from the current page.

"This is Dr. Paul, how may I help you?" A familiar laugh lightened his heart.

"What are you in the middle of that you sound so serious?"

He wanted, with all his being, to shield her from anxiety until they saw Dr. Swirsky. He wanted to, but could not, spout an untruth. "Research, Belle."

"Oh, Paul, I thought we would wait…"

"We will. It's preliminary. Nothing major." A child's voice called her attention away a moment. He swigged from a water bottle as he waited.

"How many?" she asked when she returned to the call.

"How many what?"

"I know how you are, Paul. How many browser tabs do you have open right now?"

He smiled and rested his head against his hand, making the decision not to admit the all-too-frequent research situation staring back at him on the screen. "Why don't you and the girls come into town, around four? We'll have an early supper, then some shaved ice. It'll be a splendid evening."

"That sounds wonderful."

"Consider it a date, then. Shall we meet at the square?"

"Yes. I'll look to see if any restaurants have a special tonight."

"I'll see all of my girls then. Have a good afternoon. I love you, Belle." The call ended, and he felt the sense of the surreal fall on him as a heavy blanket in winter. The eerie sensation that his life—indeed, the entire family's—would change over the summer spurred him to more researching.

Chapter 4

Once the sobering consultation was over and he was back in his own office, Paul's father reached for the phone. The sooner Autumn got into Philadelphia for an examination, the better her odds. The key would be bringing Paul around to his point of view.

Meeting his daughter-in-law touched a spot deep within his stern exterior. Admiration for the way she rose above her difficult family circumstances partially healed the rift between him and his son before their wedding. His intolerance of Paul's career choice lessened.

Despite potential for further damage to their relationship, Dr Pyoriasaari was resolute not to allow another young and effervescent woman succumb when medical help was available. He shored up his determination with a healthy swig of scotch before dialing his son. Instead, his fingers pressed out the familiar sequence for home. A more approachable expression appeared on his countenance when his wife answered the call.

"Astrid. Good to hear your voice."

"How was your meeting?"

His index finger traced the rim of the short, heavy bottomed glass. "As I expected. A young woman, with no prior history and a sudden lump. It's got the makings for a disastrous outcome. I must bring Paul around…"

"Stop and listen to yourself a moment. You cannot dictate his medical decisions any more than you can with your own patients. You give them the best information and advice you have, and they make their choices. It will be the same with Autumn."

He breathed out heavily before topping off the glass. "I dislike the side you've chosen."

She laughed. "Paul! It's the side of sense. Have you ever been able to demand a patient conform to your opinions?"

"My patients respect my opinions!" He bellowed, bringing his fist down hard enough to splash the contents of his drink on the desk blotter. "Only *my son* questions my knowledge and expertise!"

"Paavi." The endearment stalled his frustration. "Stop striving against him. He respects your opinion or he would not have called you. Respect his, and the fact that he must run his family as he sees fit." Silence reigned a few moments before she asked, in a softened tone, "Will you be home soon?"

"Yes," he said, emptying the drink. "I will call Paul, and then I will be home. I would enjoy sinking into that couch you love so much and watching one of your silly women's movies." Romantic comedies he could do without, but the comforting feel of his wife next to him, laughing aloud at the antics of the characters on screen, held the appeal.

"I would like that, Paavi. I'll be sure supper is ready when you get home."

Their conversation ended, Dr Pyoriasaari contemplated the words of his wife. The logical, surgeon's mind knew she was correct in her views. The images that haunted his subconscious demanded disagreement.

"I will reason with him. After all, he is a doctor…of sorts." He picked up the receiver and dialed.

The office manager, Lucy, announced her presence with a sharp knock. Paul turned from his screen and saw her amused expression. "Yes?"

"Your two-thirty and three o'clock appointments both rescheduled. I thought you'd be interested in case you planned to spend a solid eight hours today online."

He pushed away from the desk. "I could use a break. What say we walk to Wynter Delights and get some coffee?"

She crossed her arms. "Dr. Paul, we have a firm agreement about those sort of things."

He laughed to himself. "Yes, yes. I lost my head, forgive me. Please don't go telling tales to your fiancée that I behaved inappropriately. I want no trouble with our local fire department!"

"Not to mention your wife!" She wagged an index finger at him. "I have some old insurance claims to shred, and then I'm finished for the day. The cleaning staff comes through tonight," she mentioned as she turned away from the door.

Paul leaned back, stretching his aching lumbar muscles. "I should go see my own chiropractor," he muttered, scanning the screen to decide which pages merited saving and which were not helpful. "Lucy?"

"Yes?" her voice materialized on the phone intercom.

"Would you please make me an appointment with Dean—any morning my schedule is free."

"Right away."

He set about shutting down his computer and clearing his desk of sensitive items. A blip on his phone told him his appointment was scheduled and put on his electronic agenda. He would be certain to bring Lucy one of the expensive coffee drinks she occasionally enjoyed the following morning. Getting home early and accompanying his family into town was a treat he did not want to miss out on. Paul picked up his briefcase, and was patting his pockets to locate his keys when his phone rang. He looked at the call screen, sighed and placed his bag back on his desk.

"Hello, Father." He returned to his chair.

None of the conventional niceties were observed. "I consulted with Dr. Mahr today. I thought you would want to hear his opinion right away."

"She hasn't seen Autumn yet, how can she have an opinion?" Paul worked at holding his frustration intact, as did his father.

"Reasonable conclusions from case history and vast experience. As I'm sure you have done in your own career."

Try as he might, Paul could come up with no valid refute, so he allowed his father this concession. "I'm listening."

"I hope you will keep an open mind on treatment, Paul. You can research any options on your own." His manner shifted from concerned family member to respected surgeon. "Depending on the size and amount of surrounding area affected, you will have local versus systemic treatments. Surgery, chemotherapy. Radiation. Hormone therapies, although Autumn is hardly of menopausal age."

"On that, we can agree," Paul offered; he heard his father's chuckle over the sound of ice clicking against a glass. It seemed somewhat early in the day for his traditional late afternoon libations.

"There are others, as I'm sure you're aware. Dr. Mahr will discuss them at length with you when she sees you. I advised her of your views on medical matters."

"Warned her, you mean?" Tension and silence filled the line between the men.

"I don't wish to undermine you," his father finally said. "I thought it was wise to apprise her of your point of view…that is all. You are quite vocal about it."

The exceptionally apologetic tone his father used caught Paul off-guard. He massaged the bridge of his nose again. "Yes, you're right, I am. If there is anything else you think would be helpful for me—us—to know beforehand, would you email me? I was just leaving the office…"

"Of course. Your mother is looking forward to seeing the girls. I believe she has something special planned for them while we are with Dr Mahr."

"I'll have Autumn call Mother to confirm. Father…" Paul swallowed hard, his pride a bitter pill. "Thank you."

"You are my son; what more is there to it? Autumn is a special young woman. I do not want to see you—either of you—hurt."

The underlying, unspoken fear that there was reason someone would be hurt forced the men off the phone quickly.

Elbow-deep in a session of house plant repotting therapy, Autumn didn't hear Paul's car pull up the driveway. When he appeared on the patio, she started before rising from the project.

"What are you doing here?" She hurried to him, offering an awkward hug. "I must have lost track of time…"

"Not at all. My last two patients rescheduled. I was able to leave early. I'd like to walk into town with my girls tonight." He kissed her forehead. "And, their beautiful mother."

"Beautifully filthy! I'm almost done here, then I'll go shower. I found a Groupon for La Quinta and the new fusion place. You and the girls can decide which, either is fine by me." She smiled before walking back to the prolific spider plant, which was currently residing in four separate hanging planters.

Inside, Paul was greeted by Jacquie practicing Vivaldi on piano. She gave him a substantial hug when he joined her on the bench.

"You're playing wonderfully. When is the summer recital?"

"The last week of June," she said, tinkling a few off key notes. She frowned and corrected herself. "Mom said we're going to visit Mimi and Papi next week."

Paul folded his hands, resting them on one knee. "We are. Mimi has a special time planned for you and Emmie. I spoke with Papi just before I left work today."

Jacquie appeared to carefully study her sheet music. "Is Mom sick? Why is she going to see someone at Papi's hospital?"

Something inside Paul's chest tightened; an iron fist of anxiety. "What makes you ask that, Jax?"

Jacquie stopped playing and faced him, tears welling in her eyes. "I heard Mom talking to Grammie. She said she was scared. Mom isn't afraid of anything. She said something about a doctor and Papi's hospital." When her father didn't answer right away she looked down. "I didn't mean to listen. I came down to ask Mom for something and heard that little bit."

He took her hand. "We're going out to dinner tonight, and we're going to enjoy the evening together. We will talk later about all of this." Relief flowed through him when she nodded in acquiescence. She was a reasonable girl; mature and genuinely repentant about overhearing part of the phone discussion. "Why don't you run up and get ready for tonight. Set aside your worry." *I've enough of it for all of us,* he closed silently.

The late afternoon was beginning to cool. The family turned onto Maple Street, a side street off the main road through Lakeville, where Silas's coffee shop was located. They waved when they passed the large storefront window Wynter was vigorously wiping. Emily's attention veered to the book store across the road, clamoring over a new addition to her expanding home library.

"Not tonight, love. We're here to enjoy dinner. What was the address again, Belle?"

Autumn pulled a printed coupon from her small bag. "The next block over. It's close to the pizza shop." She returned it, then clasped Paul's hand. "It's a beautiful night."

Paul squeezed her hand. He hadn't broached the subject of speaking to the girls. The goal was for this night to be as carefree as possible before bringing them to Autumn's mother for the overnight stay. The feeling of upheaval and change clung to him, refusing to be ignored, or better yet, removed.

When they were done with the gastronomic escapade, they strolled the main street, stopping in the town square to watch a particularly intense game of chess between a Lakeville high school student and one of the firemen. The crowd applauded the outcome and the humble nature of the student when the game turned to the fireman's favor. Paul steered his family towards home, and the ice cream shop strategically placed en route.

Noticing his wife shiver, he placed an arm around her as they walked. The girls, oblivious to the chill in the air, walked ahead of their parents, discussing the virtues of butter pecan in a chocolate-dipped waffle cone versus a plain cone. Autumn slid her arm around his waist and happily sighed.

"A perfect evening. Thank you."

He gently squeezed her shoulder. "Perfect company." They shared a loving smile. "I've something you need to know. Jacquie overheard you on the phone earlier. She knows something is amiss regarding your health." Her body tensed under his touch. "I told her that we'd talk later. I know you aren't ready, but the situation bears an explanation."

Autumn's head dropped. "I didn't know she was downstairs," she muttered, kicking at a leaf on the sidewalk. "I waited until they were upstairs before I called my mother."

"I'm sure you were cautious. She came down to ask you something, heard you were on the phone and caught a small snippet of what you were saying. She was apologetic about listening, but you can't blame her. You aren't often distressed."

"I don't want them worrying, Paul. I know what it's like to be constantly concerned about a parent…the instability it can produce." She breathed in deeply. "I saw how it warped Sunnie's view of my own father. I can't have them worried over me…"

Paul pulled her closer. "Belle, that was different. He was deliberately behaving badly. We need to speak to her. Frankly, openly, but not incur fear. Emmie is probably too young to understand the gravity of it all." His pace slowed. "Do you want me to…"

She looked back up to him, a determined expression masking her own insecurities. "No. Together. As always." She took his hand. "Always," she repeated more vehemently than she meant to. Paul stopped, turned to her and wiped a stray tear from her cheek.

"Always, Belle. Always." They embraced, promise and commitment pushing back the anxiety of the situation until Emily called to them from their front walkway. Paul tightened his arms before releasing Autumn, then clasped her hand. Together. The promise stayed with them through the discussion with their daughters and into the restless night.

Chapter
5

The drive home from Strattsburg was agonizingly silent, Paul's occasional attempt at conversation stalled by Autumn. The conversation with Dr. Swirsky played over and over in her head, consuming her.

Definitely a lump... Radiation... Chemotherapy. Glad you'll be seeing Dr. Pyoriasaari, he's one of the top surgeons in Pennsylvania.

"Don't do this, Belle," she heard Paul say.

Tearing her gaze from the predictable pine scenery, she turned to him. The concern that was crinkling his eyes brought on a rush of shame. Of course he was as impacted by the diagnosis as she. She pulled in a breath, asked for a deeper well of strength, then reached for his hand.

"I'm so sorry, Paul." He grasped her hand, quickly smiling her way before returning his eyes to the road. "I've been morbid. As much as I try not to, I can't help it."

"My father has always said the emotional battle is as hard as the physical, perhaps more so. We'll get a good night's sleep, then head to Philly in the early afternoon."

She held tight to his hand. "Yes, that's a good plan. Your mother is so excited about taking the girls to the theater to see *The Lion King*. She's got a whole day planned, including dinner at her favorite place. It'll cost a small fortune!"

He laughed, a little forced sounding. "They can afford it, not to worry. I'm glad she'll have them out and occupied while we're with Dr. Mahr. I have quite a few questions I need to jot down once we're home."

They turned onto the quiet street Sammie lived on, the winding road soothing some of Autumn's angst. Spring was in full force in Lakeville, the colors vivid in both manicured yards as well as the long stretches between lots. When they arrived in the drive, she saw the girls in the yard. Emily was swinging with Aina, without care or worry. To one side, just visible beyond the garage, Jacquie stood with Sammie, face downcast. The lump that suddenly formed in Autumn's throat rose to a choking sob.

"It'll be fine, Belle. I'm glad she can talk to your mother." Paul cut the engine and turned to his wife. He took both hands in his. They were soft-skinned, but firm, confident. "We will make it through this. Take a moment; I'll go say hello to Rob." He kissed her cheek before getting out of the car. He walked around the front of the car, heading towards the deck with a wave to family in the yard. Emily called to him to watch how high she could swing. He paused, leaning against the railing before applauding her efforts. After blowing a kiss to Jacquie, he disappeared into the French doors.

Autumn bowed her head, whispering a plea for composure and alternately wondering when this well would run dry. Moments of silent communion passed, self-possession returned to a level that left Autumn feeling able to face her mother and eldest. She rummaged in her bag for tissues, swiftly wiping her eyes and blowing her nose before she stepped from the car. As Sammie and Jacquie approached, she summoned a smile.

"I'm going to make some iced tea, Sweetie," Sammie said, reaching for a hug before walking by. "Come in when you're ready." She gave Jacquie's arm a light, reassuring squeeze as she continued on.

After her mother vanish into the house, Autumn turned to Jacquie. "Let's walk a bit, I'd rather Emmie not overhear anything." Her arm slid through her daughter's and she held tight as they strolled along the side of the garage.

"It's bad, isn't it?" Jacquie asked, her voice pitched high in anxiety. Autumn swallowed hard, swiftly calculating how much to disclose to her.

"We won't know for sure that it's cancer until we have more tests taken." She felt Jacquie stiffen and her steps slow. "Dr. Swirsky is happy I'm going to see your grandfather's colleague. It's always best to have another opinion."

"But, he thinks you have cancer," Jacquie stated. Autumn stopped, turning to the girl. She had grown so in the past year. Her hair was a beautiful golden shade, the tight, childhood curls giving way to more stylish waves. Soon they'd be having "the talk" of maturation, bodily changes, the purchase a first bra. All things Autumn thought she was well prepared to share. Now she wanted to gather her in her arms and plead with the heavens to not allow Jacquie to grow up.

"Yes," she answered, knowing that anything less than the truth would make it harder for Jacquie to hear when confirmed "Yes, he does. We won't know anything else for a few weeks. Tomorrow…"

Jacquie threw her arms around her, quiet sobs releasing the fears she'd held in since overhearing the phone conversation. Autumn held tightly, allowing them to subside, listening to Jacquie's breathing steady. They stood, embracing, until Emily came running over to them. They folded her in and held tight a few moments before walking, arms linked, into the house for the promised iced tea and a brand of comfort only Sammie could dole out.

In one of Philadelphia's most tony neighborhoods, Paul Pyoriasaari, Sr. heard the car pull up in front of their restored brownstone. He rose, crossed the room and moved aside the sheer curtain when he reached the side window by the door. Emily bounded from the car and started up the steps, only to be called back by her father. They spoke a scant few seconds before she was on her way back.

A grin only she could bring about formed. "Full of life, that one," he murmured, dropping the fabric. He swung the door open before she had a chance to ring the bell.

"Hello, Papi!" Emily's arms went around his waist, youthful excitement exuding from her. He bent to kiss her head, his long arms encircling her.

"Go, find Mimi. She's making herself beautiful for your big day in town." He released her to find Astrid. He turned back as Jacquie mounted the steps. She smiled, eyes bright, holding out her arms. They hugged, kissed and greeted each other before he sent her along after her sister.

He was unprepared for the emotional wave that crashed over him, as strong as the Atlantic, when he set his eyes on Autumn. It took all his inner resources, but he managed a smile for her as she alighted the cement steps. One glance passed between them in which both immediately knew the other's fears. It was an eternal moment, over when Autumn hugged him.

"Hello, Papi." She pulled back, her smile beaming, no betrayal of their private understanding. "It's good to see you. Thank you for arranging everything."

"Of course. You'll have top treatment, I guarantee it. Let me go help Paul with the bags…" He turned without making further eye contact. In a flash he was down the steps and by the car. She breathed in heavily, then walked inside.

The girls were loudly exclaiming over something deep in the house. Autumn placed her bag on the entryway bench and headed to the kitchen. Hardwood shone, the bright white risers contrasting with the darker wood on the staircase. Fine art hung in the hallway, nothing large and garish. Gilded frames surrounded nature scenes, a park bench, a portrait of Paul's parents. Autumn passed them by without a glance their way, her sight focused on the French doors ahead.

The small yard boasted one tree, a beautiful dogwood that shaded the back portion of the urban garden. The leaves were bright green and buds were beginning to open, the pretty pink flowers making splotches of color here and there. Autumn stood at the door, immersed in its simple beauty. *"Abide in Me,"* she heard whispered into her heart. *"Abide."*

"It's blooming early this year."

Caught between listening to the inner voice and responding to the outer, Autumn turned to greet her mother-in-law. They hugged, a warm and comfortable embrace. Astrid held her at arm's length when they broke apart, studying her intently.

"You have a peace about you, dear. That is good." She patted her arms before releasing her. "The girls are very excited, I sent them to get changed. We should be on our way in an hour. The matinee show, then early supper at my favorite spot. Oh, I am looking forward to Emily's face when she sees Simba!"

As Astrid moved gracefully around the kitchen, keeping up her monologue on the afternoon's agenda, Autumn observed her. Astrid was completely opposite in appearance to her own mother, yet as open and accepting of others. She held a quiet, dignified faith, rarely sharing what was on her heart. When she did, Autumn always found it profoundly applicable and worthy of remembrance.

There was soon a plate of light lunch before her, as well as a glass of green tea, made complete with ice and mint sprigs. Autumn picked at the salad of quinoa and kale, commenting on the wonderful dressing when the men walked in.

"Ah, good, you're eating. It will be a long afternoon," Paul Sr. offered in his no-nonsense tone. Autumn met her husband's eyes, and noted the mild irritation with a small smile. They must have been having a disagreement before entering the house. Paul read her plea for peace, coughed into his hand and managed a lopsided grin for his mother.

"I hope there's more of that for me, Mother." She embraced him before handing him a plate with a more substantial amount of food than Autumn's. He sat next to her, added one of the home baked, buttered rye slices from his plate to hers and hunkered down.

"We should get to the hospital early," Paul Sr. said, bringing a plate with him to the table. Astrid sat by his side. "I thought, perhaps, you'd enjoy a tour of the facility. It's grown since you last saw, Paul. A whole new wing, new cafeteria. Quite impressive."

Paul's shoulders stiffened, a subtle change Astrid did not miss. "I don't think…"

"I'd like that, Papi," Autumn interrupted, placing a hand over Paul's. "I've never been there." She rose, taking the platter with her. "I'm going to freshen up a bit and talk to the girls before they leave." She placed the dish on the counter by the sink before hurrying from the room.

In a rare show of frustration, Astrid slapped the table with both hands as she stood. "I'm warning the both of you…do not make this a battle between you! This is not about either of you or your careers, it is about that dear woman you just chased from the room with your ongoing feud. Put aside your petty differences now." She glared at them before following in Autumn's wake.

After tossing his half eaten bread down, Paul massaged the bridge of his nose. She was right, of course, but he hadn't thought he was being ornery. Perhaps, it was time this tension between he and his father was put to rest. Not only for his wife's sake, but for all.

He looked across the table. His father waited, chin resting on the tips of templed fingers, patiently watching him instead of berating. They spoke simultaneously.

"Father, I'm sorry."

"Forgive me, Son."

Their laughter pushed the negative pressure between them out of their minds for the moment. Paul Sr. picked up the thick, hearty bread on his plate, took a man-sized bite and wagged the remaining piece at his son.

"I sense we want the same results, Paul." He wiped a stray crumb from his lip. "I do not want to argue. I will do everything that I can for you, as much as you will allow. It is your wife; she's a smart woman. I will respect your decisions. Your mother, it seems, will keep my ego in line." A wry, semi-smile appeared.

"Both yours and mine," Paul agreed, matching his expression. "I will keep an open mind. Autumn, of course, is my priority. I do appreciate your input and advice." They nodded and finished their lunch as an amiable silence— not often found between them—settled.

Autumn quickly wiped tears from her cheeks before she opened the guest room door. The smile was forced, but her mother-in-law didn't seem to notice as she slipped past. She rested a hand on Autumn's cheek. "Let's talk, dear. Don't let those fool men upset you." Once the door was closed, she led Autumn to a window seat, then settled herself on the edge of the bed. "Tell me what you are thinking."

A myriad of comments, emotions and fears bounded forward, eager to spill out and ease Autumn's heart and mind. The one she first expressed to her mother won out.

"I'm scared, Mimi. And, I hate that I am scared. I think I'm more afraid of what this will do to my faith than what it will do to my body." She sniffled before settling into the cushions surrounding the bay window.

Astrid folded her slim arms. "I understand. We are afraid to question our Maker, even though He allows it. I don't think you should worry about that; I think you know He can handle our emotions, even when…no, especially when we cannot." She rose and perched on the opposite side of the window.

Wrapping her arms around a patchwork pillow, Autumn sighed. "I know. I know that in my head, I suppose. I've been through hard things before, Mimi. This is the first time I've faced my own…well, my own mortality."

"Now, let's not run off to that! You haven't even been seen yet! Many women survive and never have a reoccurrence. They go on to live more vibrant and fulfilled lives."

"But, that's just it! I HAVE a very fulfilling life! I don't want that to change. And, there's the enormity of choosing a treatment option. What if Paul and I don't agree? How will it affect the girls?" Autumn faced the window, staring out on the street lined with brownstones and clean sidewalks.

"You will face each question when it is time. Right now, it is time to splash some cool water on your face and go to your appointment. Then, you will have more information. Until then, you will pray. And, so will I." Astrid leaned forward, took Autumn's hand, not letting go until Autumn turned back.

"Thank you," she whispered. "I'll go refresh my face. Please let Paul know I'll be down in a few minutes."

An expression of admiration crossed the older woman's face. "Of course, dear. I must make sure the girls are ready. The curtain goes up in two hours!" She rose, crossed the room, and hesitated at the door. She left with the sight of Autumn's bowed head in silent prayer ingrained in her mind's eye.

Chapter 6

Indigo

The sweeping tour of the hospital ended at Dr. Mahr's office door. Autumn braced herself for the onslaught of questions and the inevitable, uncomfortable probing. Paul, Sr., opened the door and ushered them in.

The office was not near the pristine condition of Paul's father's. A basket overflowing with magazines leaned against a table in one corner, and the distinct odor of burnt microwave popcorn lingered in the air. Someone peeked out from behind the glass enclosure at the desk. Dr. Pyoriasaari waved before the figure disappeared.

A door burst open. A small woman fumbled into a lab coat, making her appear as a child wearing a garment snitched from mother's closet. She smoothed some hair from the middle of her eye behind her ears, which instantly bounced right back to the position it had been. She stepped forward, holding out her hand in a beeline toward Autumn, her introduction equally focused.

"Good afternoon, you must be Paul's daughter-in-law. I'm so glad that you could come. I'm Dr. Mahr. Paul briefed me on your circumstance. Why don't you come this way, and we'll dispose of the necessary questions before the exam." She had shaken Autumn's hand and had an arm wrapped around her back to lead her to the inner office. "Paul, you know the way, please meet us in exam room twelve. Now, let's get better acquainted…" she said to Autumn as the office door shut soundly behind them.

Paul barely had time to pick his jaw up from the floor before his father guffawed. Dr. Genevieve Mahr was not the vision of a doctor his father would have recommended nor worked with. He followed his father across the office and into the series of hallways. Relief flowed when he saw the neat and tidy condition of the examination rooms.

"How long has Dr. Mahr been with the hospital?" He quickened his steps to match his father's stride.

"Ten years. She's the best we have. I know she appears a bit eccentric…"

"Only a bit? I admit she is not what I was expecting from your high praise. I was…well…" Paul fumbled for the correct wording as they entered the assigned room.

"You were expecting me, perhaps?" Paul Sr. leaned against the small counter to one side of the exam table, crossed his ankles and pushed his hands into his pockets. "I was very much against Dr. Mahr at first. As we worked together and her reputation grew, I came to a point where I could set aside things that I did not agree with. She's an excellent surgeon. I think that you and Autumn will be comfortable with her."

Anything Paul had to say in answer to his father's pronouncement had to wait, as Autumn and Dr. Mahr walked in. Autumn looked at ease, and stepped to his side.

"This is Paul, Dr. Mahr. Of course, you know my father-in-law."

"It's nice to meet you." She nodded her acknowledgement. "Now, let's get to the meat of this appointment. Autumn, you can step back there, yes…the curtain will close. You'll find everything you need. From the waist up is all we need right now. Paul, I assume you'll step out, initially?"

"Of course, Gen. I'll be just outside." He moved to leave, then paused, and reached for his son. An awkward, yet reassuring pat on the shoulder resulted before he exited the room, allowing for their privacy. When he closed the door, he exhaled the breath he hadn't realized he was holding, and leaned against opposite the wall. Crossing his arms, his attention remained focused on the plate bearing the number 12.

"My opinion is this," Dr. Mahr stepped back from the table, helping Autumn into a sitting position as she spoke. "That is a late Stage I or beginning Stage II tumor. It's perfectly positioned for a lymph biopsy. We can, of course, do a further examination with ultrasound or MRI. I'll order a blood draw, also. I'm ready to take any step that you want, today."

"You think this is cancer," Autumn said, gathering the light cotton fabric of the exam gown around her. Paul stepped to the table and placed a hand on her shoulder. He was unsure if it was his hand or his wife that was trembling.

"It's certainly something that should not be there. Until we remove it, we won't know, unless you choose the biopsy procedure." Dr. Mahr reviewed the options available. "I'll step out and allow you to discuss the matter. Please take your time. We'll be just outside."

"Thank you." Paul's tone was tight. When the doctor closed the door, he settled on the edge of the table and gathered Autumn to him. She clung to him as they prayed together for wisdom and direction.

"They will choose the least invasive option first."

"Which is fine, Paul. You know you must respect and accept your patient's decisions." Dr. Mahr answered on autopilot. She stood in the center of the hall, jotting notes on a tablet. The incessant clicking sound wore on the senior doctor's fraying patience.

"Please, Gen."

She looked up from the electronic version of Autumn's file. Uncharacteristic concern shadowed his face/features. This was not a fellow surgeon she was dealing with, but a worried family member. She silently chided herself for the lack of compassion, and lowered the device.

"Forgive me, Paul. I wasn't thinking. I understand how you feel. We still need to give them the room to make their own choices regarding treatment."

"Yes, yes, but if this is a fast developing strain…you know as well as I that you must be aggressive in certain situations."

She examined a nail, frowned and returned her attention to his steely gaze. "I don't disagree. We've worked together enough that you know my position. You also know that I will give my best opinion, and how I would approach it, then allow the patient to make their best informed choice. I assume you recommended me to them because you have a level of trust and respect for the way I work."

"Of course." He pushed off the wall and paced a few steps away from her. He turned, striding back to the spot he had vacated. "I do not make a good patient myself, I'm afraid. Less so, when a loved one is involved. Stepping back is proving to be…"

The door to the exam room opening stalled his confession. A familiar, yet forgotten, wave of trepidation swelled in his chest as he looked into his son's eyes. He read every fearful thought and question in them as though a typewritten page was before him.

"We're ready, Dr. Mahr. Father."

Feeling riveted by invisible, arctic bolts through his feet, he watched Dr. Mahr enter the room. Paul held the door, expectantly waiting for his father to follow. It was a moment before he was able to make his feet obey the command to move.

Autumn, still gowned, although one of the light examination sheets draped her shoulders, sat straight and tall on the table. It wasn't determination Paul, Sr., saw, it was a rare confidence. Naturally, there was fear, but the absolute calm that he observed blanket his son when he stood alongside her was awe-inspiring.

"We've decided to have whatever scans can be done today. Whichever one or ones will be most conclusive. Once we get an answer from those, we'll decide on a biopsy or removal. I…we'd like to take this one step at a time, and weigh each option carefully."

"A sensible course of action, Autumn," Dr. Mahr said, shooting a glance toward her fellow surgeon. "Why don't we get you to x-ray, then we can prepare you for a CT scan. Are you allergic to shellfish? Have you ever had a reaction to contrast dyes?"

"No, and I've never had a contrast dye test before." Autumn slid from the table with Dr. Mahr's guidance. She took Paul's hand, a common gesture that Dr. Pyoriasaari had seen before, yet this particular time it caused his throat to tighten and a salty sting to his eyes. He turned away and coughed twice, moving to follow only when he was certain he regained a tighter control of his emotions.

Never before had Autumn been unable to lie still. It took all of her focus to breathe deeply and recite Scripture as the table slid into the center of the scanning machine. *Stay still. Be still. I am Yours.. Keep still.* She repeated the litany to herself while the technician clicked and scanned and clicked and scanned.

"Great job, Mrs. P. You're finished." A cheerful voice pulled her attention. When Autumn opened her eyes, she was looking up at the ceiling of the room, not the inside of the apparatus. "It's okay to move. I'll help you up in one moment…" The young woman concentrated on the screen, pressed a few keys on the board, then rose. She reminded Autumn somewhat of her sister-in-law, who wore a similar, spiky hairdo.

"Your husband is waiting just outside. Do you feel like you need a chair? Sometimes people feel dizzy after the procedure." She smiled, her dark hair and deep hue of lipstick contrasting her light complexion.

"No, I'll be fine. Thank you, Stacy."

"Dr. Mahr ordered a rush on this, so you should have results tomorrow. I'll be sending out good vibes," Stacy said to Autumn before turning back to her work station. The benign comment caught Autumn off guard. During the long walk back to Dr. Mahr's office, Autumn pondered the state of Stacy's faith, and what she could—or should—have offered in response.

The Saturday morning rush to ballet class and Little League baseball was handled by Rob in order to give Sammie a chance to touch base with Autumn in privacy. She sat at the dining room table with her coffee, shopping list and sale flyers strewn around her. Autumn sounded plucky when she answered the phone.

"Good morning, sweetie. I'm just checking in on you. How did the girls enjoy their evening out on the town?"

"Oh, they had a wonderful time. We stayed up late listening to details of Mufasa's costume and how the waiter asked Jacquie if she wanted a cocktail. Astrid has them outside right now painting planter boxes."

Sammie grinned as Autumn supplied a few more details of the girls' adventures. She could imagine Emmie's wide eyes at the play; she was such an expressive child.

"We should hear from Dr. Mahr this afternoon," she abruptly switched topics. "I'll know more after that. I know—for some strange reason, I just know—that I'm going to do whatever I have to, to fight this. Mom, their faces last night…I can't imagine not being here for them."

"I understand. How does Paul feel about this?" Sammie strained to hear Autumn's answer.

"We need some time to talk again. So far we've been in agreement, but I don't know how he's going to react. I'm afraid he'll feel that I'm siding with his father. They've already had some tense words. I don't want my decisions to be a catalyst to their disagreements."

"I'll be praying. Please let me know what you find out."

"I will, Mom. I think I may give Storm a call. I'm feeling a little envious of the girls having this fun time together. I need some sis chat. I wish she had a furlough coming up."

Knowing the suggestion would be denied, Sammie mentioned, "You could call Sunnie."

"I know I could. It's not the same. I'd like it to be, but it's just not. I better go, Mom. I need to talk to Paul. Love you." Autumn refrained from listing the many times past that she and Storm tried to engage Sunnie, whether to join them for late night discussions or after school walks home before she moved away from Lakeville. Sunnie was a beloved sister, but she held more of a guardian and defender role in their eyes. It always had been, and in many ways, still was an odd relationship.

The conversation left Sammie mulling exactly how the past choices by various people in her life affected her present day circumstances. She looked beyond the tabletop to the wall, where current family pictures hung. Thankful her younger children wouldn't have the type of baggage the older ones carried, she went back to the mundane chores in which she derived great pleasure.

Paul was sitting on the bed, gazing out over the yard when Autumn returned to the guest room. She went over to him, leaned against his back and looked down at the scene. Several bottles of colorful paints, the yellow knocked over and pooling, were scattered across the patio table. Paul's mother and the girls were laughing over something, the delightful sound drifting up to them.

"They look like they're having fun," she said, stepping back. "We need to talk."

Though his expression did not change, she saw his shoulders stiffen. When he finally looked away from the window, he solemnly nodded. "I know, Belle."

Tears welled too quickly to stop their unwelcome arrival. "I had a hard time sleeping last night. I kept weighing all the outcomes against their faces. Paul, I have to do everything I can to fight this…"

"Dr. Mahr hasn't called yet. It may be benign. A simple surgery to remove the mass, and it's over."

"It's not benign. Don't ask me how I know, but I know. Surgery is rarely simple." She walked to the dresser and pulled a tissue from a decorative box. "As soon as you found it, I knew." She dabbed under her eyes.

"So, you're taking a defeatist attitude already?" He sat on the bed. "You'll surrender to despair and popular treatments, knowing the poisons they'll pump into your body, which cause other equally serious issues. You'll ignore the years we've spent together, researching and living as naturally as possible." The irritation refused to be masked.

"It's not that easy, Paul. And, I am not surrendering to anything! I know the time we've spent taking those precautions will help me now. Despite this tumor, I'm healthy! This is more complex than…"

He stood, refusal etched in every feature. "I will not have the argument that I have had with my father for years with you. There's no need for a discussion, since you've already chosen the path you want to walk. You'll excuse me. I'm going for a walk." Before Autumn could comprehend what he had just said, Paul was gone. She heard the front door slam closed before she sank to the floor. Tears of confusion and hurt poured out with pleas for a softened heart upon his return.

Chapter 7

The reverberating sound of the door caused Astrid to look up from her gaily painted clay pot. Nothing about the back of the brownstone looked askance. Then, from the front stoop, the sound of her husband's voice met her ears.

"Paul! Where are you going? What's happened? Paul!"

Jacquie, too, looked up from her project, her gaze focused on the bedroom window. Astrid placed her brush on the newsprint and rose from the bench.

"I'll be right back, girls. Shall I bring us back some tea and cookies?" Emily enthusiastically agreed. Jacquie nodded, returned her attention to the table and complimented Emily's smudged floral designs. Astrid hurried through the kitchen to the front door. Paul, Sr. entered, shaking his head.

"What's happened?" She caught the heavy door before it could entertain their neighbors once again, and shut it quietly.

"I've no idea! The fool boy went running out without so much as a knock on my office door!"

"Paavi, did you have anything to do with that?" She pointed towards the street. He held up both hands in defense.

"I haven't seen either of them since last evening! Why are you assuming he's argued with me?" He cast a dark look up the staircase. "I hope they haven't heard bad news from Gen. Perhaps I should call…"

"No! You must stay out of this. I will go and see if Autumn needs anything. Would you bring the tray of pips out to the girls? I'll bring some tea after I see to their mother." Astrid lightly ascended the steps.

A resigned sigh emitted before Paul Sr. turned to the kitchen. Naturally, his wife assumed it was he who had angered his son to the point of raging out of the house. It happened before. He picked up the wrapped plate of cookies that Astrid had referred to. She often made piparkakuts at the holidays. The subtle trace of orange and cinnamon reminded him of his own childhood; happy and comfortable. He set aside concerns of the moment as he joined his granddaughters, determined that they, too, would be happy and comfortable.

"Autumn, dear, can I get you anything?" Astrid called as she knocked lightly on the door. "I've got pips and tea. Do you want to come outside and join us?"

The tempting thought of forgetting everything and enjoying some of the traditional, spicy cookies passed swiftly. Autumn leaned against the bed, knees at her chin, wishing the concerned woman outside the room would quietly walk away. She longed to be alone, to have Paul hold her close and comfort her heart.

"Thank you, not now. I...I need to call my sister." She held her breath and counted. Before she reached double digits, she heard her mother-in-law walking away from the door.

"Brilliant idea." She got up from the floor and quickly crossed the room. "What time is it in Ringwood?" She pulled her phone from her purse and accessed the world clock. Storm resided in a picturesque town, a mere two hour train ride from the heart of London. The ministry her husband managed provided them a quaint row house which her expanding family was fast outgrowing. She saw it was within a decent time frame to make an international call and pulled up the phone app to talk face to face.

The technological advances that usually fascinated Autumn seemed incredibly slow in making the necessary connections. She almost sobbed in relief when it finally began to ring.

The screen lit with her sister's face. "Hi! Oh...Autumn! What's wrong?" Her expression swiftly changing from joy to concern.

"Nothing. Everything. Do you have all afternoon?"

"I knew Mom's email sounded cryptic. What's been going on?" Storm walked out to a garden area behind the house. A mossy wall enclosed the petite courtyard.

"I don't know why, but I always expect you to spout some British-ism, like 'chap' or 'mum.' When did Mom email?"

"Oh, probably Thursday. All she said about you was to pray. You know how Mom is." She sat in a chair, shooed a straying child back indoors and settled in for their discussion. "So, now tell me what I've been praying about."

Autumn recalled her life in vivid detail, from the moment Paul discovered the lump up to Astrid knocking on the door prior to the call. Storm was an especially attentive audience. When the telling was complete, the sisters stared at each other over the thousands of miles between them.

"When are you expecting the doctor's call?" Storm asked, a slightly raised eyebrow the only clue to what was on her mind. It was the familiar family trait that signaled any emotional response ranging from displeasure to disbelief and beyond.

Autumn glanced at a bedside clock. "Probably a few more hours. Why?"

"You should go wash your face and then find Paul! How can you sit there? You need to be of one mind before that call comes in!" The eyebrow arched a bit higher. The familial expression of exasperation hit an all-time high.

"Don't you pull a Sunnie on me!" Autumn gave a huff of annoyance, another habit shared with their eldest sibling. "I could have called her for this reaction."

"Apparently, you need it. Get off your buns and go find your man. He's as hurt, scared and confused as you are. Where would he be?"

That was a big question; one she wasn't certain she could answer. It suddenly came, and along with it, a peal of relieved laughter.

"The bell. He went to go see the bell. How could I have forgotten about that?" Autumn carried the phone to the bathroom across the hall. She set it on the counter as she searched for a wash cloth, giddy that she'd realized where Paul had gone off to.

"Hey! I don't want to stare at the ceiling, as nice as it is." Autumn repositioned the phone to give Storm a better view. "Thanks. Once you and Paul make this right, what are you going to tell the doctor?" A drop of water splashed onto the phone, blurring the screen.

"I'll text you when I know. Right now, I'm taking your humble advice to get off my buns. I should freshen my mascara." She wiped the screen clear, her fingers lingering on Storm's image. "I really miss you."

"Same here," Storm responded, a catch in her vibrant and deep tone of voice. "I'd love to be there for you…with you. Maybe I can get some time and come home in a few weeks."

Autumn rolled her eyes. "Right. Leaving Steve to run the ministry and handle your brood? I think not. Unless Mary Poppins has arrived at your house and you neglected to tell me."

"Ha! Don't I wish sometimes! No, no magical, musical English nannies have knocked on our door so far. I'll keep my eyes open, though." She grew serious again. "Listen to me. I know this is a wild roller coaster ride, but you have got to stay firmly planted."

"Why do you always think you can tell me what to do?"

"Because I'm older." Storm shot out her tongue. "So there. You know it's the reason you call me."

Autumn grinned. "I guess so. Thanks for listening and straightening me out. I'm going to go find Paul. I'll let you know as soon as I hear from Dr. Mahr."

"You better! I won't be able to sleep tonight. Hug Paul and everyone else for me."

"That's a guarantee. Love you." The sentiment was returned, then the screen went dark. Autumn rushed back across the hall, refreshed her mascara and eye liner, scooped up her keys and bag and hurried down the stairs.

Bustling crowds at Independence Mall ignored the man sitting on a bench moodily staring at the tower of the historic hall. Paul had walked around the bell, around the expanse of the whole site. Emotionally exhausted, he'd been sitting in the same spot for over an hour.

There was something about the bell's famous flaw that always resonated with him, even as a youngster on school field trips. *What is my flaw?* He leaned forward, elbows on his knees and clasped his hands together. *Why is it that I cannot accept that traditional medicine could also have benefits?*

He never envied the success his father attained. He appreciated the upbringing it secured him, the comforts some of his friends had not enjoyed. It was the expectation that he would walk the same path that others in the family trod before him that he bristled against. Experiencing horrendous medical care during his stint in the Army solidified the choice to go into natural medicine. The disdain of family, especially his father's, hardened his view against conventional healing methods.

Now, faced with the threat of cancer in his beloved wife, he knew he was at a crossroads of sorts. Could he, would he, humble his heart and accept that there were other methods, that he might not agree with, but could be the best for their situation?

"Why is this so hard?" he breathed out to himself, bowing his head. "Is it so important for me to be correct rather than my father? So much that I'm willing for the cost to be Autumn's life? God, forgive me." The weight of worry began to lift, the grip of fear loosened. "Help me to be strong. Help me to be humble." As his confessions and supplications continued, peace rested on him.

With relief that he had been able to release the burden, he sat back. People were still sightseeing, families pushing strollers, couples strolling along with clasped hands. The earth had not stopped spinning—life was continuing on. No one had been curious about the man on the bench, in prayer. He pulled his phone from his pocket, intent on calling Autumn to apologize.

Before he could dial, his attention was drawn across the mall. The unmistakable figure of his wife emerged from the crowd, obviously searching him out. Paul's heart dropped, sure of why she had come to find him; Dr. Mahr must have called. He adjusted his glasses before rising, ready to accept whatever news was about to be announced.

Their eyes met; Autumn smiled and began to walk towards him. Their pace quickened, culminating in an embrace in the center of the crowd.

"I am so sorry," he whispered in her ear.

"Me too." She pulled back and brushed wavy hair from his forehead. "Let's go back, Dr. Mahr should be calling soon. I'd like to be somewhere safe, with you by my side."

"She hasn't called yet? But…when I saw you, I thought…"

"I had to come, Paul. I don't want to argue, to have this hanging between us. I knew that we wouldn't agree at first, but I hoped we could talk it out. I realized I was expecting you to agree with me without having that conversation. I understand that I'm asking you to trust in something that you haven't trusted in for many years."

"I want you to know, Belle, right here and now. I intend to stand with you and how you choose to treat this." A sheepish grin formed. "I suppose the stubborn, prideful apple falls fairly close to the tree it sprung from." The smile he received in return felt like warm sunshine.

"It's the strong and stubborn side that becomes my protector. I need that strength, even when we disagree."

Paul slid his arm around her waist and started walking them in the direction she had come. "You have it. Always. Maybe we should stop for some cheesesteaks before going back to my parents. I haven't had one of those in ages." He winked at her. "It may be a good time to completely disregard any and all dietary beliefs as well."

Both restored to a better frame of heart and mind, the couple briskly walked across the mall and blended into the crowds.

Awakened by his absence, Astrid rolled over and glanced at the bedside clock. It wasn't yet midnight—it was unlike her husband to be out of bed. Although, it had been an unusual day, filled with tensions and distressing tidings. Paul and Autumn, after a long, weepy discussion with their daughters, had retired early. Not long ago, before she drifted into a light sleep, she heard her son check in on them, and then head downstairs. His father was wearing a groove in their luxurious bedroom carpeting. The Pyoriasaari men were not resting easily this night.

"Paavi, stop pacing," Astrid called to Paul, Sr.. He turned, shrugged his shoulders and walked over to the bed. He sat heavily, scrubbing his face with one hand.

"I'm sorry to have woken you. I am not used to being on this side of a diagnosis."

She reached over, her hand resting on the small of his back. "I know. Pacing won't change it or help you to help them through it. Lay down. Let that busy mind rest."

A deep rumbling sound, his amused chuckling, made her smile. He tucked himself into the bed and pulled her against his side. "I know what you're trying to do, my dear. My mind will not rest until after the surgery. However, a few games of racquetball tomorrow will help me think more clearly."

"Invite Paul." She felt him tense at her suggestion. "He needs some mind clearing, too. I think it would be beneficial to you both."

He settled himself deeper into the pillow. As he considered issuing the invite, he saw the wisdom in offering his son the comfort he needed in a setting that was comfortable for them both. Visions of a new, closer bond between them, that could be nurtured to grow, appealed to him. Placing a distracted kiss on her head, he mumbled, "Yes…I think it may just be."

In the room down the hall, Autumn disconnected from a tear-filled phone conversation with her mother. Paul had disappeared somewhere in the lower level of the townhouse, giving her ample time to discuss the diagnosis and the next steps on the path they would be taking with Sammie.

She relived the day with her mother: the argument, the reconciliation. How within the hour that they had arrived back after their impromptu outing, the phone call came. She and Paul were braced for the worst news. She told Sammie how Dr. Mahr patiently explained to the couple that the tumor was indeed cancerous, but contained. It was, she assured them, the best form of breast cancer with the most successful treatment options. Dr. Mahr was positive, once the removal and agreed upon protocol was through, Autumn would be declared cancer-free.

Mother and daughter shed tears of relief over that news before Autumn went on. The surgery would be scheduled before the end of the week. After all, Dr. Mahr had explained, while she could pressure the labs to rush on the diagnosis, she had to comply with the hospital's many and varied needs. Autumn explained each procedure in detail, a way of conquering the fears that arose from the thought of them. The biopsy to test the surrounding lymph nodes before removal of the tumor, to be certain that no other part of the breast was affected. Chemotherapy, to kill any errant cancerous cells that might remain.

As unnerving as the conversations had been, both with the doctor and her mother, Autumn was relieved that a lumpectomy was the first step. It would give her time to straighten out their schedules and plan meals, care for the girls, and arrange help during those trying days of chemotherapy. She rose from the bed, paused, then returned to the spot she had just vacated. Unsure of when she would again have some time alone, she began to pour out all the fears and questions, and to ask for even more abundant stores of supernatural peace and patience during the trial ahead.

Chapter 8

Astrid's thick slippers cushioned her steps from the bedroom and down the stairs. She heard her son go down hours ago, but not return. He was probably on a computer, researching. As she suspected, Paul sat at the kitchen table. Before him was not an electronic device, but an old photo album, the cover bare at one corner. He slowly and intently turned the yellowed pages.

She walked up behind him and laid soft hands on his shoulders. A melancholy smile accompanied the memories from the pictures he was perusing. Before walking to the stove, Astrid quietly asked, "Tea?"

He turned a page. "Thank you, no. I've enough adrenaline in me to keep me awake."

"You sound very much like your father right now." She bustled behind him a few moments, preparing her cup. When she joined him she leaned forward to look at the photo he'd stopped to examine. Standing beside a deep green pool, surrounded by soaring pines stood a young, strong Paul, Sr., and a beautiful woman with hair the color of freshly ground coffee. His Aunt Karin's glowing countenance brought the faded picture to life. Her arms were clasped around his waist and her head tossed back in joyful laughter. Paul Sr., young and open, bore an astonishingly similar smile.

"That was the summer we met," Astrid's hushed voice reached Paul's ear. "He caught my heart with that smile. Your aunt, she was such a joy to be around. She made me feel like I belonged from the moment Paavi brought me home to meet the family."

Paul removed the fragile photo from the plastic casing, bringing it close to his naked eyes. "How long?"

Astrid drew deeply from her cup, memories both hard and wonderful rushing at her as she contemplated the question. "We were married the following summer. Your father had started his residency. Suddenly, Karin began losing weight without cause. Your father thought it may have been diabetes, but the testing proved otherwise. She quickly moved to stage four. It was only months after that."

The fist of fear held a stranglehold on Paul's throat. *Months.* His mother had just confirmed his aunt only lived months after diagnosis. This woman, who made the flat picture surge with life--who brought something to his father's demeanor, something he rarely glimpsed.

"I want to say something, my son, then I will retire." When he lowered the photo, she could see the plethora of emotions; trepidation, confusion, anger at the inability to help. She placed her hand on his arm.

"You were named not only for your father, but for a character from the Bible. He was known for his strong opinions—he felt he had a holy calling.

Your namesake had difficulties with the ones who walked alongside the Master. They did not trust him. What is it he said? 'I need to be all things to all people.' He learned to work with what people thought, and not offend. The Apostle accepted the customs of people. I think, at times, we also need to accept ways we may not agree with, for the greater good. Please, son, think about this."

A half-grin quirked one side of his mouth before he leaned forward and kissed her cheek. "Thank you, Mother. I will contemplate what you've said."

"Spoken as a true Pyoriasaari." She ruffled his hair and rose from the table. Moments later, he heard a door softly close.

Paul's gaze returned to the picture, mesmerized by the aunt he never knew. What had that laugh sounded like? Did she dream of being married, having a family? Was she a woman of great faith before the diagnosis or had she found her faith during her illness? There were so many unanswered questions about Karin Pyoriasaari. And, one thought melded them together in Paul's mind: would someone ask these same questions about Autumn one day?

Over a light breakfast of bagels, cream cheese and fruit, Paul Sr. invited his son to join him on the racquetball courts. Paul accepted after a brief back-and-forth over missing church, unsure of what prompted this monumental show of solidarity.

"You can meet us at Mindy's Café after services, like we usually do," Astrid suggested. "We'll have lunch, then you can be on your way. I know Autumn is anxious to get home." She looked across the table. Autumn agreed both to the plan and wanting to get home soon after.

The girls immediately got caught up in discussion over the brunch menu options. The men left the table to prepare for their round of competitive stress release. Hopeful to discover some abandoned clothing left over from college days, Paul opened the closet in the guest bedroom his daughters were occupying this visit, formerly known as his. He chuckled at the sight of neatly arranged storage cartons. He found what he needed in a box containing what his mother had labeled 'Sweatpants and Gym Attire.'

"At least I had the same taste in clothes then as I do now," he said, thankful that nothing outrageously out of date was found inside. Pleased that the sizes had remained static, he changed, closed the closet door, and went to meet his father.

The club his father belonged to was not as exclusive as he expected, but it was adequate for their needs. Greeted warmly by every attendant and staff member they met, Paul Sr. led him through the complex. "I brought you a few of my older racquets to try out," he said as he opened the door to the reserved court. He set the gym bag down, removed his warm-up jacket and began a series of stretches.

Paul tried out the feel of the equipment before deciding on one particular racquet. "Do you mind if I warm up a bit?" he asked.

"Not at all. You'll find a good stash of balls in the bag. Extra gloves, too."

Watching his father go through what was an obvious ritual of stretching and jogging from the line to the wall and back, Paul began to feel as though he was in for a rough game. It had been some time since he played competitively in any sport. Outside of family walks and isometrics, he was not as active as the older man was.

"Well, I'll just have to do my best," he said under his breath. He began to hit one, small, pink rubber ball against the wall, then another, and another as a bizarre sense of already being beaten set in. *Perhaps, when we get back home, I should revisit the application for the country club.*

"Very good match, son! You're better than I expected!" Paul Sr., who hardly looked as if he broke a sweat, was putting his racquet back into its zippered case. "Let's stop at the juice bar. My treat." His offer was magnanimous, as the loser customarily bought the post-game round of refreshments.

"Fine," Paul agreed, making every effort to breathe deeply and not appear winded. A two-year trial membership to the Lakeville Country Club was sounding better with every easier breath he took. He concentrated on collecting the few stray balls on his side of the court.

In the small and brightly lit cafe, Paul enjoyed a protein smoothie; Paul Sr. sipped on a wheatgrass and spinach concoction. The silence between them was comfortable. He hated to disrupt it, but he wanted to have a frank conversation with his father. Paul placed the glass on the table before him.

"I'd like to know how you feel about the surgery." He folded his hands and looked earnestly at Paul Sr. "I admit, I am…frightened."

He forced himself to remain patient. His father was forming a response, and taking his time about doing so. Neither man wanted to upset the other; this first completely open discussion was new territory for both.

"As a seasoned surgeon, I agree completely with Gen. If it has to be cancer, this is the best possible scenario." He finished his juice and set the glass aside. Leaning across the small table, he fixed a serious look on his son. "As a father, I, too, am frightened. As a man who lost someone precious to him once before, I am frightened both with you and for you. I never want to go through that pain again. Nor, do I want you to."

"Father, please. If you think that is even a remote possibility, I need to know."

He saw the familiar and anxious expression that so many husbands of patients had worn before him. The parade of hope, the sneaking doubt, the raw fear. Yet, he knew that his son had something more, something seated well within his being. It gave him the confidence to speak candidly, much more so than to anyone at any time before. "I do not think so, Paul. Not with Autumn. It looks about as good as it can."

Paul leaned back in his chair, his visage taking on a complete transformation. For his father to confirm that this was not as grave a diagnosis as some was a relief he could not put into words. He removed his glasses and pressed the heels of his hands to his eyes. Paul Sr. cleared his throat, indicating he had more to add. Paul regained his composure, wiped his face on a spare hand towel, and gave his father his full attention.

"That does not keep away the anxious thoughts all family member experience. I lack the simple, yet deep faith of your mother and your dear wife. I've seen the same in you, as well. I think that even with this, the best cancer diagnosis possible, that you have to pull now from that deep faith and rest in whatever it is that you will go through. Cancer is never a simple disease to treat, nor does it favor one over the other. I've witnessed too much to not share your fears."

A deep breath taken, Paul Sr. admitted something he would have liked to stay buried in his heart forever. "I would very much like to share in this deep level of faith you have, Paul. I'm certain it would make my job easier to bear when things do not go as I would like." He swallowed and in a tone heavy with emotion and regret, said, "I think it would help me to let go of the misgivings of the past, too."

His aunt's smiling face emerged in his mind's eye. The question that had been in Paul's head most of the day rolled out of his mouth with no warning. "What did her laugh sound like?"

An amazing occurrence took place, one Paul never expected to unlock with that one unassuming question. Stunned to silence by it, Paul Sr. attempted to answer in his usual, clinical way, but could not. His memory banks broke free and the more he thought about Karin, the more urgent it seemed to talk about her. It was time, he realized, to release and not to fear.

"When Karin laughed," he said, as tears began streaming, "it was like the angels joined in."

He saw a shadow of his beloved sister in Paul's smile. They spent several hours together as Paul Sr. reminisced, and he was sure he felt her joyful spirit had joined them.

"Where is Daddy?" Emily tugged at Autumn's skirt, a habit leftover from toddlerhood that she couldn't seem to break the girl of. She folded the last shirt pulled from the dryer and placed it in the suitcase.

"Please don't pull on my skirt, sweetie. He and Papi are playing racquetball. You need to go upstairs with Jacquie and make sure you have all of your things together before we leave."

"But, he's taking so-oooo long. We won't get to see Grammie. I wanted to see Claire ride on Aunt Sunnie's horse and pictures of Uncle Jude's new dogs." Emily spun in a haphazard circle as she voiced her protests.

An edgy unrest was beginning to spread through the family. Autumn expected a behavior challenge in Emily with the onslaught of sweets and late evenings the past few days had included, including worries about her mother. Autumn, herself, was tired and wanted to get home, and wondered what her husband was doing out so long. She had gotten a brief text message about missing lunch, and that was all.

"Emmie, you need to stop whining. Go be sure your room is neat and the bed is made. Now," she added when Emily began to balk.

"You're being mean just because you found out you're sick!" Emily turned and hurtled from the room, wailing over the perceived injustice of life. "I want to go hoooome!"

Shocked by Emily's outburst, Autumn felt unable to contend with her eight-year-old daughter. Too many thoughts formed a maelstrom of confusion. They weren't even immersed in the battle, and already defeat stood at the door, waiting to crash in and smother her. She abandoned the packing and rushed out to the garden.

Astrid witnessed the scene and was torn between who to comfort. Her deliberations were brought to a swift conclusion by the entrance of her son and husband. Although happy to see signs of their newly-evolving relationship, she quickly explained what had just transpired.

"I will go speak to Autumn," Paul Sr. volunteered. He placed his gym bag on the washer. "Go, comfort Emily," he said to Paul. "She needs her daddy."

He walked past them to the yard. Paul stopped to peck a kiss on his mother's cheek and hurried up the stairs.

"Well," Astrid said to the empty kitchen, "I suppose I'll put on some tea."

He quietly entered the bedroom after his knocks were unanswered. Paul's heart constricted at the sight before him: Jacquie's arms wrapped around Emily as she cried. He stood silent, drinking in the picture, reminded of how much was at stake for the family in this trial they had just begun walking through.

He knocked again, louder this time. Jacquie looked over her shoulder and with a simple glance, begged him to join them. In no time, he was on the bed, his girls enveloped in his arms. When their emotions were depleted, Paul disengaged. He looked from one to the other, pleased with the young women they were becoming and mindful of the children they still were.

"I know this has been a very hard weekend for you both. I am so, so proud of you." He paused, smiling at them and caressing Emily's cheek. "We all need to be strong for Mom right now. If you feel scared or angry, please come and tell me. Even better, pray. Let Jesus know how you feel. He will be there for you, just as He is for Mom."

"I want to go home," Emily warbled.

Paul pulled her onto his lap. She snuggled in close. "I know you do, and we are. I spent some extra time with Papi today. It was something we needed to do, and I am very glad I did. Once he was very scared and angry, just like you are now."

"Was Mimi sick, too?" Emily sat up, her curiosity overriding the need to weep. Paul transferred her to Jacquie's lap. "I'll be right back," he said and exited the room. When he returned, the worn photo album was in his hand. He leafed through to the picture that had captured his imagination.

"See this? That's Papi…"

"That's not Papi! That's you!" Emily cried out. "Who is the lady you're hugging? It's not Mommy!"

"That's Papi and his sister," Jacquie corrected. "Look again, Emmie. This is an old picture."

"Why don't we know Papi's sister? Does she live here?" As always, Emily was full of questions.

The girls looked expectantly at their father. He moved to the headboard and leaned back on the pillows. They followed, and nestled on either side. Emily pulled the photo album to her lap and stared at the picture.

"She's not…she's in heaven. Papi loved her very, very much. Aunt Karin became sick, not long after this picture was taken. Because of that, Papi became the best doctor he knew how to be to help other ladies who were sick, too."

Jacquie looked again at the picture. "Was he able to help her…Aunt Karin?"

Paul shook his head. "She was very sick. He did learn everything he could about her illness. Knowing what he does, he is very sure that Mommy is going to be fine. He also told me that it's normal to be sad or mad. He was sad and mad when Karin got sick."

"Did he cry?"

He ruffled Emily's hair and kissed the top of her head. "Of course he did. He loved Karin. He misses her. Sometimes, things don't work out the way you want them to."

That was enough for the girls to absorb, Paul felt. Emily clutched the album to her chest and stared across the room. Jacquie leaned her head against his shoulder. Moments later, she asked, "Can we pray, Daddy?"

It had been longer than Paul could remember since Jacquie called him that. The circle of his arms around them grew the slightest bit tighter as they bowed their heads together in supplication for the woman who bound them all together.

When the door snapped closed, Autumn turned, hoping to see Paul. Her father-in-law laughed aloud at the startled expression she was slow to hide from him as he approached.

"Sorry," she offered, wiping the back of her hand across one cheek. He patted her shoulder tenderly.

"I know I was not who you were hoping to see, and that is perfectly understandable. Paul is upstairs with the girls. I'd like to talk with you, if that is all right."

He held out an arm, inviting her to join him to sit by the dogwood tree. She followed him over to the bench underneath the expanse of branches. When they sat, he further surprised her by taking her hand.

"When you arrived, I saw your trepidation. I also saw how you were hiding it from your family. I have seen it for many years, now. But, I also saw in you something I've only seen in few others through the years. What I saw, this quality—I have seen it in you before, but I never understood it."

He paused to watch a pair of jays squabble over a spot beside a freshly opened bloom amid ones that were already wilting. "My sister, Karin…she had that same foundation of faith. An inner tranquility," he continued, not taking his eyes from the winner of the coveted place among the blossoms. "At the time, I did not understand it. I was drawn to it in my wife. My son, he also possesses it. I think all this time, I have been jealous."

He turned from the blue jay to Autumn. His free hand enclosed the ones already clasped. "Until today. I've had a good discussion with Paul. I want to thank you."

"Thank me?" Mystified, she moved toward him the slightest bit. "For what?"

"For opening the channel of communication. Between Paul and myself. For my beautiful granddaughters. I thank you for being a woman of high moral fiber, who is a match for my son and not a burden." He made a grumbling sort of sound, embarrassed that he had gone on. "Ah, listen to me. I came to offer comfort and, here, I am taking it instead."

"Please don't feel that way. I'm glad you said those things. I *was* scared. Frightened like I never have been before. But, I did feel a peace that was hard to explain. I know this is not going to be easy or simple. Thank you for all you've done." She leaned in and hugged him.

"I do think I've come to believe that Karin was also at peace. Even through her worst pain, she smiled." He squeezed her hand. "I am confident that you will beat this in a grand way, Autumn. I will pray that for you."

The self-reliance was gone from his tone. A calm, focused assurance emanated, resting on the simple act of prayer. Autumn shed fresh tears, thankful she was able to witness this tremendous change in a heart that she had prayed for.

Chapter 9

Autumn climbed into the tub and sunk into the fragrant bubbles, happy to be back in Lakeville, in her own home, her own bathroom. These were her first quiet moments of the week, where she contemplated many of the possible outcomes the weekend might have held. Dr. Mahr could have read the results wrong. Perhaps they were altered due to being rushed through the labs. She sank under the water, expelling the manufactured worry with a breath when she emerged.

She began to outline her pre-surgery weeks, the checklist growing exponentially. She silenced her overactive thoughts with a thorough hair washing. She wished the tension and doubts would drain away with the excess water.

Stepping from the tub, she patted off residual moisture and tucked a towel around her. Autumn wiped condensation from the bathroom mirror before she began to work a wide-toothed comb through the thick, wavy hair that she usually dried straight. Not today; she was in no state of mind to fuss over such things.

The ritual continued, the plastic gently tugging through the tangles. The towel dipped, threatening to slide from her frame to the bath mat. She rearranged it before she looked back at the mirror. Autumn stepped back and allowed the towel to drop to the floor.

She knew the feel of the lump—she'd monitored it more since Paul discovered than she wanted to admit. Carefully examining the reflection, she considered her figure. She turned from side to side, noting some muscle that could be tightened up and where to find contentment with what the good Lord has gifted her with.

Autumn looked hard at the full frontal reflection. She imagined how it would change if Dr. Mahr's diagnosis proved wrong and what she would feel if the day arrived that the image might be altered forever.

How would Paul feel if a mastectomy was needed? Would his desire for intimacy decrease? What if they were to be blessed with another child? Could she ever breastfeed again? Where could a one-sided nursing brassiere be purchased? Would reconstructive surgery be feasible? If so, would Paul's father be willing to take her case or take a consultant role, or recommend someone else?

She clapped her hands to her ears in an attempt to block the questions assaulting her. Autumn turned from the reflective glass and rushed from the bathroom. She clung to the image of the young, healthy woman she was…for now.

Throwing open the closet door, Autumn pulled out the first item whose color was appealing in that moment. Building an outfit around the chosen blouse, other pieces were tossed onto the bed before moving to the dresser. A drawer was yanked open and an automatic choice of panties flew through the air to join the other garments. The following selection--bras which were arranged in attractive, neat rows--stopped her short.

An irrational sense of anger swelled. She enjoyed few indulgences, the upscale lingerie store being her favorite. It was an infrequent treat to spend a few hours alone amid the bright silks, racy underwire selections and more sedate every-day wear. After the darlings of the venture were purchased, the clerk wrapped each one in purple tissue and placed them in a signature white vellum bag. Paul was always appreciative of the evening fashion show.

"Why?" Autumn leaned on the dresser. "Why can't things just stay the same? Why, Lord, why did you choose me to go through this? I've never done anything…"

Shocked silence reigned for a moment. Where was this lack of trust coming from? How could she so brashly question the deity she so devoutly trusted? Firm belief that her life was held in His capable hands was foundational to her existence. Amid a whirlwind of conflicting emotions, she closed the drawer without extracting a foundational garment.

Autumn tugged on her clothes and looked in the mirror once more. Her clothing revealed nothing. No one would notice a lack of support. An irrational idea bloomed; her mouth quirked up in a grin.

She returned to the closet and extracted two white vellum bags from a small stash. She walked back to the dresser with new purpose. The offending articles were stuffed into the bags and deposited back in the farthest corner of the closet. Their former owner would decide which manner of disposal best suited them at another time.

Coffee that automatically brewed was waiting for the keeper of the house to make her mid-morning entrance. The ice maker chugged out a fresh batch of cubes. Quietly humming, the dishwasher cleaned yesterday's dishes. The confines of her efficient gourmet kitchen held little comfort for Victoria. She poured the steaming brew into her favored mug and wandered through the kitchen to the three-season porch. Her ancient dog lay on a well-worn bed near the mudroom. He opened one eye and watched her, faithfully, if sleepily, guarding her way.

Victoria stared into her garden, seeing nothing of the beauty she normally reveled in. Instead she recalled walking alongside her best friend during life's more devastating blows. She cried, argued with and comforted Sammie and her children often through the years when her first husband's behavior was out of control. They rejoiced when he repented and found faith, and mourned his death only three short years later. Time for celebration arrived again when their children became engaged and Victoria stood with Sammie as she joined her life with Rob's.

Breathtaking blooms of evening primrose danced in a light breeze, attempting to catch their mistress's attention. The heavy coffee mug lifted and a sip was taken mechanically, a trace of plum lipstick left behind on the rim. Flawlessly shaped brows furrowed over the sharp, gray eyes. Another time of testing, stretching of personal faith and physical challenges hovered on the horizon for the Young family. Another opportunity for Victoria to bear Sammie's burdens.

A warm and gentle hand upon her shoulder beckoned her away from the deep concern that held her thoughts captive since Sammie's call. She leaned back, assured that George's strength would be there to lean on, spiritually as well as physically.

A tree swallow swooped into a feeder that overflowed with the special mix Victoria provided her feathered visitors. The couple watched him indulge before he flew back to whichever tree in the enormous yard he called home.

"You look a thousand miles away, my dear." George's arm crooked around her. "Why so glum?"

"I'm worried. This is different. It's one of Sammie's girls. I'm already emotionally involved. What if I can't..."

"Pshh. Victoria MacDougall Reiger saying 'what if'? I never thought I'd live so long."

His teasing tone soothed some of the deep, emotional upheaval in her soul. Victoria patted his hand.

"This whole scenario brings up the nasty side of my own bout. I don't know why." As she turned to him, she shivered. "When we met, I was already two years cancer-free. You missed the worst of it. I don't relish anyone going through it, especially not someone so close to me."

"You know yourself, dear, that even the bad points have their place. You tell your group that all of the time." George caressed her arms and offered encouragement by a light squeeze. "I'll go refresh this for you. Then we'll hash it out." He took the heavy mug from her and walked into the kitchen. He returned in moments, with a matching mug in hand for himself.

George placed them on the rattan coffee table and issued an invite. "Come. Tell me what's troubling you." The well-worn wicker groaned under him when he sat.

"I wish I could pinpoint the cause, dear," she said as she perched beside him. "I hesitate to say I have a premonition. I just have a horrible...instinct, I suppose...that this will not be an easy road for Autumn." She sighed and leaned back into a comforting arm.

"It may be. You know that no diagnosis is guaranteed to be a simple surgery or, on the other hand, years of chemotherapy. You've seen them all."

"I think that's what troubles me most. I've seen the joy when the diagnosis is wrong. The pain when it becomes hard. Women who survive, only to have their marriages fall apart. If I could spare her any or all of it..."

"You've never spoken like this before, Vi." George drew a long sip of his coffee.

"It's never been so close to me. I simply cannot lose perspective, but this is Autumn. She's like my own daughter! I feel that I've not ever fully understood the fear a mother has when her child is diagnosed. Every terrifying thought and possibility. This is all brand new territory. How will I be able to help Sammie through this, too?"

"You've always said she's an incredibly strong woman. I'm sure you'll draw whatever you need for them both. You always have." He pulled her close. They sat a long time in silence, joined by their ancient Irish wolfhound. Cadfael limped over, stiffly laid at George's feet and huffed out an enormous doggy sigh.

Victoria spoke quietly, so as not to disturb their canine guest. "Do you recall our third date?" She turned her head to view his expression. The mention of the momentous occasion drew a wide grin. "How could I forget? It's not often you are challenged to love someone who is not 'complete' in the middle of the Lakeville Country Club's Grand Dining Room."

A hint of pink colored her face. "I was a brash fool. I couldn't believe you asked me on another date after that, much less proposed. Thank you for never shrinking away." She entwined her fingers with his.

"I know that was your moment—to discover if I would love all of you, even if some of it was what you considered unattractive. I told you then, Vi. There's more to a woman than a cup size." He kissed her forehead.

His nap disturbed, Cadfael gave them a scruffy look of scorn. He hoisted himself up and lumbered back to the quiet confines of the kitchen. George patted her hand before rising, and collected their empty mugs with a swoop of his hand.

"Why don't you make that phone call you've been putting off? Invite Autumn to lunch, with the girls and Samantha. You can break away to have a private chat with Autumn at some point."

Victoria smiled up at him. When she stood, she hooked her arm through his. "You always know exactly how to pull me up out of the pity party I can easily get lost in. I'm so glad I married you." They walked to the kitchen, parting ways with a kiss before Victoria unplugged her bejeweled phone from the charger.

"Mom?" Autumn heard Jacquie call from the kitchen. "Mom, Mrs. Reiger is on the phone, can you talk?"

Autumn pulled herself from the bed and glued a smile on, hoping her furious and confused thoughts wouldn't be apparent. Jacquie was still chatting with Victoria when she entered the kitchen. Thanking her daughter when the phone was handed over, she breathed in deep and feigned composure.

"Hello, Vic. Nice to hear from you."

"I hope I'm not disturbing you, dear. I'm calling to invite you and the girls to lunch one afternoon next week. It's been ages, and I'd love to catch up with you."

"Next week? Let me check my planner; what day were you thinking?" She pulled a thick book across the counter and leafed to the specified week. Victoria suggested several dates. "Thursday will work. Can I bring anything?"

Autumn pulled a pen from a zippered bag, and recorded the event with purple ink. She waited, pen poised to jot down more details.

"Not at all, dear. I thought I'd see if your Mom and Aina were free to join us as well. We'll see you then." Her disconnect was as abrupt as the conversation. Normally Victoria chatted about the grandchildren she longed to visit, or, at the very least, inquired on the general health and well-being of her family.

Perplexed by the odd conversation, Autumn placed the phone down and took the planner and bag to the table. The current monthly and weekly layouts were blank, except for the newly planned luncheon. She looked over to the phone again, then back to the page open before her.

"If I only knew when the surgery was going to be scheduled," she muttered as she dumped supplies from the bag and began marking off tasks in a rainbow of ink colors, adhesive flags and decorative washi tape.

Paul arrived home after 5 to find Autumn still at the kitchen table, surrounded by pens, menu sheets, a tablet, index cards and a stack of mail. She was busily filling in various boxes in the appointment book. It was a familiar sight, although the level of intensity was elevated.

"Been busy?" He placed his keys on the table, then slid off his jacket. "Did you pick up the dry cleaning?" Her blank and somewhat frazzled stare spoke louder than words.

"Never mind that, I can swing by the shop tomorrow at lunch. What's on the dinner menu? Should I light the grill?"

Her mouth moved, but no sound emerged. Paul moved the chair next to hers and sat. He pulled her hands to his lap.

"How long have you been at this?" He tipped his head towards the table.

"Since Victoria called." She decided not to admit to how early in the day that had been.

"How is she?"

"Who?" Autumn glanced back at the pile. "Paul, I need to get back to this…"

He pulled her from the chair and walked her to the sliding glass door. "Look out there, Belle. Have you been in the garden today?"

"I just told you, Paul, I spoke to Victoria, then I started working on my monthly plans. I always do…"

"You don't always spend the entire day planning. Has Dr. Mahr called with a date?" She shook her head. "Then, what in the world are you so busy with?"

"Meals. Appointments for the girls—physicals, eye exams and dentist. A bulk shop and cook weekend. Scheduling bill payments. The normal things."

"Yes, all normal tasks, but you do not normally try to accomplish them all in a 3 week time span! I've never seen every block on your pages filled." He opened the door. "Out. Now. Go put on your gloves and dig in the garden. I'll take care of dinner."

When she looked at him, he was certain she somehow felt betrayed by his direction. Her chin quivered before she turned away, leaving him alone in the kitchen. He prayed she would find solace outside as he went about dinner preparations.

Tromping across the small yard gave her a modicum of satisfaction. "I can't believe he threw me out of my own house!" The shed door was tugged open. "He ordered me out here like…like…like my brother telling his dogs what to do!"

A pail was taken off a hook, and dropped at her feet. Into it was thrown a trowel, shears and a cultivator, followed by gloves. The metallic clanging filled a primal need to be loud and obnoxious. Picking up the bucket, Autumn left the shed and went to the garden.

It wasn't an urgent situation, but it did need tending. The gloves were pulled on, repositioned and settled. She surveyed the plot, chose a patch by the pole beans and went to work weeding, aerating and pruning. Amid the scents of the earth and clipped vines, away from her family, she was able to release despondent tears.

Chapter 10

Midnight

"Mommy's been outside a long time." Emily's face was firmly pressed to the door. Milky lip prints marked the otherwise clean surface. "Isn't she coming to tuck me in?"

Paul glanced at the clock. He'd been polishing the same stainless steel oven handle for 14 minutes. He put the dish cloth down and pushed his glasses up the bridge of his nose.

"Not tonight. Go put your nightgown on and brush your teeth. I'll be up momentarily. What book shall I bring?" He knew the question would peel Emily away from the door and worry over Autumn. She ran over and hugged him.

"The mouse and the cookie. No…the dog and donut. Yes. The dog and donut book. Thank you." She began to hurry toward the steps, then abruptly turned back. "The pig and pancake. That's my favoritest." She smiled brightly and continued on.

A sticky note was quickly scribbled and stuck on the microwave where Autumn's dinner awaited reheating. He spared a quick look to the garden before eliciting help from Jacquie on the whereabouts of the requested story books. She quickly found all of the titles Emily had suggested and accompanied her father upstairs.

When Autumn came in, the kitchen was empty, clean and glowing golden from the setting sun. What she heard as she walked across the room lifted her heart—Jacquie and Emily's laughter over Paul's voice. Her eyes misted over when she read the note. Instead of warming her dinner, Autumn removed it and placed it in the refrigerator.

She went upstairs to her bedroom to discard the dirty clothing and don fresh, bright yoga pants and a comfortable tee. She washed quickly, afraid to miss another moment of the fun happening in the other room. The mirror held the same reflection it had earlier in the day. Autumn looked, brushed some loose locks from her forehead and smiled.

"I will not miss another moment of this party you call *life*, Lord. No matter how much longer You have for me here, be that weeks or years." She tossed the washcloth in the sink. The cheers and hugs received when she entered Emily's room removed the lingering heaviness that tried to reclaim a portion of her heart as its own.

"I would have never given the pig an Irish accent," Autumn said to Paul. "Emmie obviously thought it was a splendid idea!"

He closed the door to their room. "I'm sure I've heard Silas read it aloud that way. It was a fun evening. I'm so happy that you joined us."

"I couldn't help myself. I felt so alone outside. Then, I had to question myself. Why was I shutting everyone out?" She shook her head. "I feel like a split personality the past few days. I don't know if I'm going to laugh or cry from one moment to the next. I dislike the sense of losing control over the smallest things."

"It's normal, Belle. Please, though, don't shut me out." He emptied his pockets, depositing items on a chest of drawers. "By the way, I put all your paperwork in your sewing room."

"I'm sorry that I left a mess for you to clear up before dinner. Thank you for taking care of it all for me." Autumn fluffed pillows and smoothed the sheets after turning down the bed. The small accent pillow she had made years before flopped off the edge of the bed and onto her foot. She looked down at it a moment, then back to her husband. He was in the midst of changing, unaware of the wild urge to laugh welling up inside of her. She hunched down, scooped up the pillow and launched it across the room.

The missile found its target, neatly knocking the shirt from Paul's hand. When he turned, Autumn was seated on the bed, not-so-innocently scrolling through books on her e-reader. He arranged his expression, careful not to snicker or otherwise look amused as he walked slowly to the bed.

"Going to read?" His hand hovered over the corner of his pillow.

Autumn looked up, started to answer and was soundly conked on the noggin by a king-sized, down-filled implement of doom. Abandoning the reading device to a safe corner of the nightstand, she snatched her pillow, holding it before her as a shield and crouched on the bed, ready to pounce. "Bring it, mister. I'm warning you, one thing I excelled at in my youth was pillow fighting. Ask my sisters."

Paul backed up to the dresser, picking up the bomb Autumn had first hurled. He tossed it back at her, and made his attack while she was preoccupied with the smaller projectile. The counter strike was swift and thorough; Paul was crying for mercy in less time than he estimated. They fell on the bed, laughing long and hard.

Autumn leaned on his chest. Her face was flush, and her eyes were bright, full of life and love and happiness. For the first time since the discovery of the lump, Paul was confident that she would come away from this stronger. He could not only see the new, deeper resolve; it radiated, touching and revitalizing the recesses of his own faith.

Paul reached for her, tunneling his fingers through her hair. He imprinted every detail of her beauty at that moment onto his heart. "I love you," he whispered before he pulled her close to offer congratulations on a battle well fought.

Breakfast dishes were washed and sitting in the drying rack. Jacquie was practicing for the recital and Emily was in the process of completing a video math lesson. Autumn gathered her cleaning supplies, ready to head to the bathroom upstairs when the phone rang.

A cheerful greeting reached Dr. Mahr's ears. She hoped the balance of the conversation would remain so. "Good morning, Autumn. I'm calling to let you know when we've got your surgery scheduled."

"I wasn't expecting to hear from you directly," Autumn said, discarding the cleaning bucket and walking toward the office.

"Usually the hospital scheduler would call. I wanted to touch base—how are you?"

Autumn grinned as she reached for her agenda. "I'm doing fine, Dr. Mahr. Thank you. What date?" Choosing a hot pink Sharpie pen, she waited on the response.

"I've got you in on Thursday, June 2, at nine. I tried to push it up a bit, but that was as soon as we could get." Irritation sounded in the doctor's voice.

"That's fine. Do I need to do anything beforehand?" Autumn circled the date and wrote out the details in the square.

The doctor's demeanor changed. Autumn was amused, recognizing the same take-charge attitude and confidence Paul exhibited when talking to patients.

"Of course, there are the standard consent forms to sign. I will email those to you. If you bring them with you, signed, that is fine. They will detail your diagnosis, surgery procedure, everything we have discussed. You can have all of your pre-operative testing done at Dr. Swirsky's office, no need to make a trip to Philadelphia for that. My office will send all that to him. Also, nothing to eat after 8PM the night before. Are you planning on staying the night with Paul?"

"Yes. My mother will keep the girls here at home. Paul and I will be at his parents' home the night before."

"Very good. If there is anything else, I will call. Be looking for an email. I will see you on June second."

When the call ended, Autumn punched out a group text message to family. She ignored the immediate incoming messages to dial Paul. She read through several when Lucy at the office put her on hold.

"Praying, sis!" arrived first from both Jude and Storm, practically simultaneous. Typical to-the-point responses from them, Autumn thought as she scrolled through the list. All you need do was ask for prayer, and she knew that Jude and Storm would be on their knees.

"I can watch the girls and/or send my cleaning ladies over. Let me know which you'll need more," Sunnie chimed in. She was always the first to offer help, either physical or financial. Autumn was always astounded and grateful for the generous additions Sunnie regularly made to the girls' bank accounts.

"Will cook up a batch of your favorites," came from Wynter followed by a long prayer from Silas that filled Autumn's eyes with tears and her heart with peace. She heard Paul on the line and abandoned the remaining messages.

"I heard from Dr. Mahr. June second is the big day." Her voice broke.

"I'm going to assume that news is what's blowing up my phone with text messages. It doesn't take your family long to get the prayer chains in various churches working. Did you call my parents?"

"Not yet," she admitted, reaching across the desk to the tissue box. "I wanted to talk to you, first. Dr. Mahr asked if we'd be staying with them. I wonder if she's spoken to your father."

"I don't think HIPAA would allow for that, even in this circumstance. I'll call when we're done." He paused, a million emotions fighting for prominence. "How are you?"

She laughed, wiping the tears away. "I'm fine. Excited and nervous. Glad to finally have a goal, of sorts, to reach. It still feels surreal, like I'm watching this all play out from outside of myself."

"Did you have plans for dinner?"

"Yes…" Autumn flipped to the daily agenda page, ready to announce the night's menu.

"Change them. I'm taking you out. We can leave Jacquie in charge for a few hours. Do whatever it is you need to do to prepare them, then put on your best dress."

Leaning back in Paul's ergonomically fitted chair, she laughed aloud. "A hot date with you tonight and lunch at Victoria's later this week. This is turning into a grand adventure, and not a cancer scare."

"That's exactly how I want it to stay, Belle. No fretting, no more tears. I'll call you when I'm on the way home."

"I'll see you then, Paul. Love you." She placed her phone on the desk, picked up a red pen and drew a large heart around her evening time block. She continued to color it in and add an arrow with a black pen. When complete, she examined the artwork, laughed to herself and shut the planner. She left it on Paul's desk to begin one of the girl's favorite crock pot dinners, macaroni and cheese with butter cracker topping.

"Dr. Pyoriasaari's office, this is Elliot."

"Hello, Elliot, this is Paul. Is my father available?" Paul rarely used his father's cell phone during office hours, a habit he appreciated Autumn followed suit with. There was nothing more irritating for both doctor and patient than unwelcome interruptions.

"He's almost finished with a consultation. Would you like me to check, or shall I have him call back?"

Paul weighed the options. "If you would, please slip him a note—let him know we have the surgery date, and to call me when it's convenient for him. I would appreciate that."

"Absolutely, Dr. Paul. Would you mind my asking for the date? I will put it in his agenda right away."

It took Paul a moment to respond; in the years that Elliot worked for his father, he was never referred to as "Doctor," nor had Elliot been so amiable. There had always been a level of aloofness Paul could not penetrate.

"Umm, certainly. June second."

"June the second," Elliot replied in a low voice. "It's on his calendar and I will give him this immediately. I hope it all works out for the best."

"Thank you, Elliot. We're sure that our Lord has us in His hand." The phone went abruptly silent, so much so that Paul thought he offended Elliot to the point that he disconnected the call.

"I'm not certain what transpired when you were here, Dr. Paul." Elliot responded as Paul contemplated hanging up himself. "Your father…he's been very different around the office. He's been humming one certain song every day, almost continually. When I asked him about it, the doctor said it was his sister's favorite hymn. I've worked in this hospital a dozen years," he continued, unable to contain the need to discuss this very recent shift in his work atmosphere. "Most of those with Dr. Pyoriasaari, and today is the first time I've heard about your aunt. I think your wife has touched his heart in a very profound way. I…well, I thought you should know."

Paul coughed away the lump that formed deep in his throat. "Thank you, Elliot. I appreciate you telling me. We'll see you in a few weeks."

"I'll get him this message stat. Have a good day, Dr. Paul."

Sinking a bit deeper in his chair, Paul locked his hands behind his head and contemplated the conversation. "My wife," he whispered. "She's really something special."

Chapter
11

The word *home* conjured up many differing emotions for Autumn. The long and secluded driveway leading to Victoria's house stirred pleasant and awful ones alike. Coming to Victoria's was the same as coming to her own childhood home except this was arriving at a safe haven. Autumn pulled her van beside her mother's car and shut the engine.

When they stepped from the vehicle, Emily hurried up the wide porch steps. Sammie stepped out of the door to greet them and was quickly enveloped in Emily's exuberant hug. Images of past painful greetings at Victoria's doorstep temporarily flooded Autumn's mind.

"What's wrong, Mom?"

Autumn turned to Jacquie. "Nothing." Squeals emitting from inside the kitchen made both look toward the house. Close in age, Emily and her young Aunt Aina behaved as cousins.

"You had a funny look," Jacquie persisted. "Almost like you were going to cry."

Reaching back into the van, Autumn picked up her purse. "It's nothing but pesky memories that are better left in the past." She closed the door and started toward the porch. Jacquie followed, understanding that her curiosity would go unsatisfied.

The gourmet kitchen was always a delight for Victoria's guests and today was no exception. The island counter was gaily decorated. Small Mason jars overflowing with bright peonies were set at each place. Victoria's penchant for making every casual gathering an event did not go unappreciated. Both Aina and Emily ooh'ed and aah'ed over the woven placemats, linen napkins adorned by beaded rings and brightly patterned salad bowls.

"Did you make spisghetti, Miss Vic?" Emily's inquiry was answered with light laughter from all.

"Not today, sweet one. The menu today is strawberry chicken salad. I remembered that you enjoyed pink lemonade spritzers last time you visited. Would you and Aina fill this with ice, please?" Victoria handed the child a blue tin.

The girls hopped from their stools and hurried to the refrigerator. Soon the sounds of ice cubes plunking into the bucket filled the kitchen.

"Can I do anything, Miss Vic?" Jacquie asked. Victoria directed her to fill the glasses. Jacquie poured frothy pink liquid from a beautiful cut crystal pitcher.

Autumn excused herself to the bathroom. Sammie and Victoria shared a concerned glace between them before the girls brought ice and drinks to the table. When Autumn arrived back, they began to dish up lunch after blessing the meal and their time together. Conversation was light and enjoyable. Victoria entertained them with a string of escapades in her various volunteer work. Sammie shared the somewhat hectic schedule of a proud ballet and baseball mom. Aina and Jacquie compared their respective upcoming recital dates, and Jacquie offered to play her selections over dessert.

"That would be lovely. George finds little time to play these days. I would love to hear you."

"Why don't I get these dishes cleared away? I'll put out the coffee mugs, too." Sammie began to pile bowls and collect flatware.

"I'll help, Grammie." Jacquie started a pile of linens.

"Autumn, I have a new feeder that is attracting hummingbirds from miles around. Would you like to see it?"

Before her mother could accept or decline Victoria's invite, Emily piped in. "May I come, too? I love hummingbirds!"

"Emmie, I'd rather you help Aina with the cookies. She knows where Miss Vic keeps her pretty platters. We'll take a walk out back after Jacquie plays so you can see the hummingbirds." Sammie smiled at her granddaughter, which resulted in acquiescence on Emily's part. Once a bag of snickerdoodles was placed in her hands, wildlife viewing was forgotten.

Sensing the conspiracy at hand, Autumn joined Victoria to walk toward the gatehouse set 500 paces from the farmhouse. She saw the feeder, a multi-level contraption that smacked of space travel, as they approached. Autumn took a breath and asked, "What did you want to talk about, Vic?"

A throaty laugh proceeded the answer. Victoria hooked a slim arm with Autumn. "Your mother and I are quite transparent, aren't we? How are you, dear?"

"I'm fine. I suppose as the surgery gets closer I'll feel a bit nervous. I'm better now that I have a diagnosis and a plan of action."

"That's good to hear. I've been praying since Sammie first called me." They paused to enjoy the show of miniature, jewel-tone birds darting about in their feeding dance.

"Has Jude seen this?" Autumn asked. Her brother's backyard was becoming a veritable wildlife sanctuary. No animal or bird was unwelcome, including the black bears native to their area.

"Who do you think installed it for me? With Steven over in Europe, I rely on Jude for construction and mechanical projects."

An emotional laugh escaped Autumn. "I could use Storm home right now."

Victoria squeezed her in a one-sided hug. "I'm sure. I want you to know that you can come to me. I've stood where you are standing right now. Without the system of support that you have. It wasn't socially acceptable to discuss things such as breast cancer at that time."

Autumn wondered what Victoria—a woman she knew for years and considered family—would think if she closely inspected her figure. A deep pink flush rose at the thought of violating another person's intimate space.

"I...I didn't know, Vic."

"It's not the normal dinner topic. For many years, I told no one. Only George knew, and that's an altogether different story…"

"Tell me." The one question that plagued her rose. "How did you deal with that? I'm so worried that Paul will have a negative reaction after." The pink deepened to magenta.

"George handled it better than I ever did. Come, let's sit," Victoria pointed to a bench not far from where they stood. As they walked to it, the hummingbirds scattered at the sound of their footsteps.

"We were only dating a short time. Three dates, to be exact. I was several years out from my cancer. Steven was a baby when I was diagnosed. I knew the moment I met George that I would marry him. But, I was afraid." That was a monumental confession for Autumn to digest. "I can't imagine you being afraid of anything, Vic."

Victoria waved her hand. "I was very insecure at that time in my life. I'd been through a terrible early marriage, an even worse divorce and battled cancer all before the age of twenty-five. I was a single mother who was marred for life and no man would ever find me the least bit attractive again. Damaged goods, both physically and emotionally. My father was the mayor; we all had to keep up appearances. I wasn't allowed to be vulnerable, especially in a public forum."

It was unimaginable that this woman, who stood strong in her beliefs and never wavered, could have felt the way she described. Autumn sat mesmerized by the tale.

"By our third date, I knew I had to bare all to him. Figuratively, of course. I was afraid of what he would say, or not say. It panicked me to think the man I was so attracted to…so certain we were meant to be…could very well never call me again. I was so distracted by all the negative that I blurted out the truth over dessert. 'George,' I said, 'have you noticed that I only have one breast?'"

Stunned silence lasted only a brief moment. Autumn opened her mouth to comment, realized it was moot, and laughed. Victoria grinned, folded her hands and set them on one knee. Autumn gestured for her to continue in between breaths.

"Yes, I did. That dear man, he wasn't even flustered. His gaze never wandered below my chin. He took my hand and looked me direct in the eye. 'A man who judges a woman by what's filling her blouse rather than what fills her mind doesn't deserve a woman as wonderful as you. Vi, there is more to a woman that a cup size.'" Victoria's countenance softened, her eyes shimmering with a sheen of tears brought on by the precious memory. "Six weeks later, we were married. Our wedding night was the most beautiful, magical experience. I was whole again."

Unaccustomed to openness of this depth from Victoria, Autumn leaned forward and hugged her. "Thank you for sharing that with me."

"I do have my motives," Victoria said. "Of course, I want you to know that I understand what you'll be going through. Please, do not hesitate to call me. I mean that! Any time, night or day."

Autumn held her hand up. "Promise."

"I host a small group here every other month. Women in various stages of the disease and survivors. Some from town, church, the surrounding area. I'd very much like for you to come. Our next meeting is in July."

"I think that would be good for me." Autumn agreed. A new admiration for Victoria bloomed. They discussed details of the surgery on the way back to the house.

With the one concern she held onto fallen to the wayside, Autumn determined to replace every piece of lingerie she'd abandoned. She was not going to allow this challenge to drive a wedge where none existed.

The weeks dissolved into days, then hours. A teary early morning departure from Lakeville on the first day of June weighed on Autumn as she lay in bed at her in-law's home that evening. Astrid kept the temperature at a comfortable seventy degrees, but for a mother with a concerned heart, she felt chilled to the depth of her soul.

She pulled the down comforter up under her chin. *How I wish I could have a bowl of ice cream,* she thought. *It wouldn't help me warm up, but...*

Paul entered the room, shutting the door behind him. Autumn counted 3 DVD cases in one hand, and a portable player in the other. He placed them all on the bed before he went to their suitcase on the window seat.

"I know it's not ice cream," he apologized, pulling sleep pants from the bag. She laughed at his apparent mind-reading abilities. "Since we can't snack, we'll watch some old comedies. Pick which one you'd like while I change."

She reached for the cases, examining the titles and back matter before choosing an all-time favorite. She waved it at Paul when he walked over to the bed, and he grinned. "I just knew you'd pick that," he said, pulling the player toward them.

"It's classic," she countered, opening the case and passing him the disc. In no time they were humming along as Gene Kelly and Donald O'Conner, in outrageous white and green checkered suits, declared how fit they were.

"Count backwards from 100," the anesthetist instructed Autumn. His tone was calm and confident.

She began to recite a psalm. "I love you, O Lord, my strength. The Lord is my rock and my fortress..."

Dr. Mahr watched Autumn's lips move in silent supplication. When she was certain Autumn was fully under the anesthesia she looked over to the observation window. She gestured to the family members to pick up headsets.

"Can you hear me?" she asked when it appeared both had them settled and comfortable. Paul and his father waved. "Very good. Paul, you understand this is a professional courtesy. I want you to be apprised as the surgery progresses."

They nodded, father and son, both holding a similar and grim expression. Dr. Mahr turned her full attention to her surgical team. "Are we ready?"

Affirmative responses soothed the nervous tension in the room. Every surgery was the most important, all risks were the most grave. When a surgeon lost the wonder of the power they were allowed, and the skills they were gifted with, things could turn bad in the blink of an eye. Pre-surgery jitters were a normal, expected and swiftly dispelled portion of the time. In a decisive gesture, Dr. Mahr pulled the lighted mask down and signaled the team for the surgery to begin.

"Move, son."

Paul started at the touch of his father's hand on his shoulder. He pulled one ear free from the headset. "Pardon?"

Without taking his eyes from the action on the other side of the great window, Paul Sr. repeated, "Move. You've been standing in one position too long. I don't want you to faint. Move your legs. You know better."

The inclination to argue diminished as quickly as it rose. "Thank you for reminding me. Do you want some water?" He pulled the headset off and set it on the hook.

"No thank you. Walk the hallway twice. That should restore the circulation. It looks like Gen has removed the tumor. Our pathologist is examining the margins before Gen closes. She cuts a much closer margin than I do." He turned from the scene to see his son's expression change from optimism to worry.

Embarrassed, Paul Sr. coughed slightly. He had gone on as though he were instructing a first year resident. "I'm sorry, Paul..." His head snapped back to the glass. "Say again, Gen?"

Paul abandoned his walk and snatched the headset back. Replacing them was too much trouble. He held it to one ear in time to hear Dr. Mahr repeat herself.

"We need a re-excision. The margin was not clear. You know how these things can sometime go. You always tell me that I don't take enough." She looked over to the window. "Please don't be concerned, Paul. The lymphs are all fine. Autumn is doing well." She nodded before turning back to the table to begin the second phase of the surgery.

Engrossed in what was happening in the operating room, Paul missed his father leave the observation lounge. A strong hand on his shoulder moments later pulled his attention away. Paul Sr. handed him a bottle of water and slid a chair to his side.

"Sit. Everything is in hand. Would you like me to page the chaplain?"

The crack of the bottle opening was the only sound. Paul swigged from it before answering. "No," he said. "No, I'm sure he has other, more serious things to deal with. Prayer is an excellent suggestion. Would you like to pray with me?"

With the flush of embarrassment for a second time that morning, Paul Sr. pulled the other chair he'd procured next to his son's. "I will allow you to lead. I am far too new at this to be as eloquent as your mother."

"God doesn't mind simple prayer, so long as it's from the heart. Jesus once asked, who was more righteous; one who stands on the corner, beating his breast and announcing his holiness to all who pass by or one who simply asked for forgiveness, because he knew he was a sinner. Mother may be more eloquent, but her prayers are from her heart. It will come to you, too, as you get to know Him better."

"I look forward to that," Paul Sr. said before bowing his head. Father and son joined hearts as Paul prayed for the ongoing surgery to be successful.

"The margin is clear."

A round of triumphant, yet subdued, congratulations were expressed by the team before they zipped back into action. A pre-threaded suturing needle was placed in Dr. Mahr's hand.

"Did you hear that, Paul? It's clear and we are closing." She began to place microscopic stitches inside the exposed flesh, repairing the deepest layer first. "I will discuss the next steps with you as soon as I am finished."

"They can't hear you Doctor. They…well, it looks like they're praying," an assistant in the room said, mystified by such behavior from the senior surgeon. The new-found faith he exhibited was quite curious to others. Several stopped what they were doing to gaze at the sight.

"People, stay focused!" Dr. Mahr commanded. "I know you don't often see Dr. Pyoriasaari outside of his role in this hospital. He is a man of very deep convictions; that he would pray with his son should not surprise anyone. Now, pay attention to your situations. I won't have any incidents in here due to gawking at men who are depending on our care of the loved one currently in our hands."

Abashed, those who momentarily lost perspective refocused. The room was quiet as Dr. Mahr completed the final sutures. She lifted the loupe from her forehead, switching off the light. "Please dress this," she directed, "then bring Mrs. Pyoriasaari to PACU. I will be along after I complete my notes and talk to the family. Thank you all. This is a job well done."

The team performed their final duties while Dr. Mahr transcribed her notes on Autumn's surgery into her tablet. She removed her surgical garb, washed her hands and sponged her forehead. Her usual prepared statements would satisfy neither man awaiting news.

"Okay. It's a good thing it's mainly good news," she muttered. She swiped her fingers through damp hair, straightened her scrub top and marched out of the operating theater.

Paul and his father were conversing quietly. They both rose when the door opened. Dr. Mahr brusquely launched into a detailed narrative of the surgery. Paul Sr. folded his arms across his chest and listened intently. Paul stared into the operating room; Autumn had already been taken to the recovery area. A crew filled the room, meticulously disinfecting every surface and tool used.

Paul Sr. sensed the private chiding in Dr. Mahr's report. No surgeon willingly admitted they were overly confident or had made an error in judgement. "Don't be hard on yourself, Gen." He laid a hand on her shoulder. "As you said, everything was clear after the second excision, and the lymphs are all good. It was a simple..."

"May I sit with Autumn now?" Paul interjected. "I'd like to be there when she starts waking."

"Of course." Dr. Mahr nodded to her associate, irritated over the swift dismissal. "Paul, you know the way. I will send you my notes."

"Thank you, Gen. I'll come by your office after I escort Paul and look in on Autumn." He offered a paternal pat before dropping his hand. He would pacify Dr. Mahr once he reunited the couple.

Dimmed lighting, digital beeping and quiet voices dominated the post-anesthesia care unit. Nurses on duty greeted Dr. Pyoriasaari and one pointed him in the direction of Autumn's cubicle. Paul moved the curtain aside and slid into a chair next to the bed. He grasped Autumn's hand and bowed his head. His father scanned the computerized chart during the private moment. The nurse assigned to Autumn's care soon joined them in the compact space.

"Good day, Dr. Pyoriasaari. You daughter-in-law is doing fine." Paul Sr. moved aside as he began recording vital signs on the screen next to the bed. "I'll bring some warm blankets in a moment. She should come around before I get back. There's an emesis basin, should it be needed, right under there." He pointed to a table in the corner beside Paul.

"Thank you, Charlie." Dr. Pyoriasaari shook hands with him. "How is the family?"

"Thriving, sir. Bethany is set to graduate this summer. Thank you for her letter of recommendation." He completed recording vitals, signed off on the chart and went on to the next patient.

"His daughter is in our nursing program. Bright young woman. She'll give her father a run for his money." Paul Sr. chuckled, then asked, "How does the dressing look?"

Paul pulled the gown back and examined the wound site. "Good, not too swollen; minimal bleeding. Nice stitching technique, too. There should hardly be a scar. Autumn will be pleased about that."

"The tumor was in the right spot. It was easy to get at, and if dimpling occurs, it won't be noticeable. She shouldn't need padding except for comfort during healing."

"That's good. Very good. I can't thank you enough, Father, for all that you've done. For just being here for us." Paul extended his hand. "Nice working with you, Dr. Pyoriasaari."

With a great smile, Paul Sr. clasped his son's hand. "It's been my pleasure... Dr. Pyoriasaari."

A low moan broke the moment of bonding, and both men focused their attention on Autumn. Her eyes fluttered, then she blinked. "Paul?"

"Right here, Belle," he said. "How are you feeling?"

"A bit nauseous. Can I have some water?" Her voice was hoarse. "I'm chilly."

"Charlie will be right back with some heated blankets. It's good to see you. I will get you some ice chips before I go see Gen." Paul Sr. leaned over the bed. "You're our star patient today. Once the medications wear off, you'll feel sore. Lay still and let Paul pamper you." The faint lines at the corner of his eyes crinkled when he grinned.

"No worries," she whispered. "I plan to." She tried to smile back. Just as Charlie returned with blankets, Autumn succumbed to the nausea. Despite his valiant efforts, Paul ended up needing to change.

"Charlie, please get Autumn some Zofran, and send a message to Elliot to bring a set of scrubs from my office immediately." Paul Sr. entered the medication order on the electronic chart. Charlie left the cubicle on his mission, tapping out a text message as he walked away. He was back in no time and administered the pill. Autumn laid back, feeling weak. Paul Sr. gently brushed hair from her face.

"The Zofran will relieve the effects from the anesthesia. It may only last a few hours or several days. I'll make sure Gen gives you a script before you leave." He bent to kiss her forehead. "You rest, now."

"Thanks..." Autumn mumbled. The medication took swift effect and she was soon sleeping. Elliot showed up soon after with the requested surgical clothing, a hospital identification lanyard and toiletries in a canvas bag stamped with the hospital logo. He asked about Autumn, and shared a few pertinent scheduling updates with Paul Sr. before returning to the office.

"Elliot does think of everything. Why don't you go change? I will stay with her until you return. Leave your clothes in the bag, I'll take care of them for you."

Paul gladly took his father up on the offer. He kissed the back of Autumn's hand before he rose and picked up the bag Elliot left at the foot of the bed. Paul laid a thankful hand on his father's shoulder before leaving Autumn's side.

Satisfied with the readings on the monitors, Paul Sr. settled on the foot of the bed. He closed his eyes, recalling Karin's surgery experience. He felt the now-familiar sting of loss, but he was able to smile at the other, cheerier memories of Karin—her effervescent personality and the way she had of making those around her feel cared for as they cared for her.

He looked down at his daughter-in-law. "I must thank You for allowing Autumn to have the opportunities Karin did not. I ask You, if I may, to watch over her and my son. They still have much to walk through." The neophyte prayer was reverently and ardently whispered.

"The incision was closed and dressed at 10:46 AM. The surgery was an hour and forty-six minutes duration." Dr. Mahr tossed the recorder on the desk. "Why did I not take a larger margin? I shouldn't have been so...argh." She abruptly rose and stalked around the room.

Thinking through every moment of the surgery, Dr. Mahr concluded that she hadn't made a bad judgement. Working alongside Dr. Pyoriasaari on many occasions constituted a different parameter. She had been keenly aware that he was observing, not as a fellow surgeon, but as a family member. One who had more knowledge than most.

"That had to be it," she mused, pacing across her office to a prolific fiddle-leaf fig in front of a southerly facing window. She examined the leaves. "It was a routine procedure. Well, as routine as one can be. Yes..." She lifted a withering leaf, running her thumb across it. "I think you need more water."

She turned from the tree at the sound of a deep chuckle behind her. Paul Sr. walked into the office. "I'm sorry, Gen, I didn't mean to eavesdrop." His face held a bemused expression.

"Would you like me to copy my notes or shall I email them?" She ran fingers through her hair—a habit that rarely yielded the desired results.

"Email, please. I would like to offer an apology." He paused when Dr. Mahr's mouth dropped open. "I did not want my presence to cause you any discomfort. I'm afraid I accomplished exactly that."

Her chin jutted forward. "I'd be lying if I said it didn't. I only just realized it, myself. I think that may be why I misjudged the margin."

Paul Sr. waved away her comment. "You did no such thing. It was a fine procedure. I recommended you because you are the best surgeon in this hospital. Your penchant for bearing your soul to a houseplant notwithstanding." He winked. "I did prescribe some Zofran. I told her you would be sure to give her a script. When will you release her?"

"I see no reason she can't go home tomorrow. You know I like my patients to spend the night, regardless of insurance companies complaining over the cost. She can start the chemotherapy in a few weeks. I'd like her to come back for the initial treatment, then her local doctor can monitor." They discussed the protocol Dr. Mahr had chosen. "I anticipate four rounds. Unless something aberrant shows in the lab work, we got everything. Of that, I am certain. It was the most contained tumor I've seen to date."

They'd had similar discussions over numerous patients for years. Why did she feel he would disapprove, castigate or ridicule? He stepped forward and clasped her on the shoulders.

"Thank you, Gen. Autumn is in the best hands, both in heaven and here on earth. I will leave you to your ficus tree. Get some rest. I will offer prayers of gratitude for your skill daily." His smile was warm. Something tender and deep shone in his eyes.

"Thank you. I appreciate that." She paused, then said, "Whatever has happened to you, Paul—and I know something has—I'd like to hear more about it."

A smile brighter than any he'd given to date appeared. "I will be happy to, sometime soon. Perhaps you and Bill can join us for church services one Sunday, then dinner at our house. It all started with my sister..."

She knew she was gawking, however, Dr. Mahr couldn't help it. "Your sister? Paul, all these years, I didn't know you had a sister."

"I know. I have done her and myself a great disservice by not speaking of her. I will check with Astrid and let you know when a good weekend is to join us. Thank you, again." He left Dr. Mahr to speculate among the leaves.

Chapter 13

A Hint of Cerulean

The fifteen-minute drive from Lakeville to his fellow chiropractor's office afforded Paul a minor amount of solitude in these newly hectic days. Autumn's chemotherapy took over every free moment of the family's time, whether it was going to the appointments or helping Autumn through the first few days following.

Reflecting on the undesirable side effects of her treatment was not the way Paul wanted to spend the drive. He pulled up a podcast from the last men's retreat he attended and set it to play. The speaker's voice filled his ears and his heart began to settle. He reached his destination in a much better frame of mind.

He was met at the office door with a crushing bear hug. Dean Merino, by all accounts, had been the star of the college wrestling team in his days at Penn State. Banners, trophies, blue lion heads and framed newspaper clippings decorated the walls of his office. He often joked that his wife preferred them there than in their own home.

"How are you?" Dean asked as they walked to the exam room. "Come, tell me how Autumn is faring. Is my recipe helping?"

They stepped into a room and Paul removed his dress shirt. He pulled the belt from his slacks and emptied the contents of his pockets onto the counter. "I'm fine. Autumn swore me to secrecy about her true feelings over that concoction of vitamins and minerals you suggested. I do have a picture to show you," he grinned as he scrolled through the images on his phone. "It will tell the whole tale."

They laughed at Autumn's expression; she glared at a blender filled with a deep green liquid. Paul laid his phone by the rest of his belongings and laid face down on the adjusting table.

The former wrestling champion examined and adjusted Paul with a light touch. "You're very tight in here," he said, kneading the muscle below Paul's right shoulder blade. "Don't forget the stretching we learned. That will keep you from tightening up here."

"Time seems to be at a premium these days. My routine is as compromised as Autumn's has been. She'll miss Jacquie's recital tonight. It's been a sore point in the house. Thankfully, my clients are understanding and no one has left me to come to you." He winked. "I will make some time in the day for isometrics and stretching. We put in an application at the club, too."

Dean's heavy eyebrows arched. "Really?" He kneaded a bit deeper in a different area.

"My father…he's got me interested in racquetball, of all things. My father-in-law loves basketball, tennis, golf. All the in-laws play basketball. It's never been my sport. Racquetball has a certain, I don't know…grace and skill level that appeals to me."

"I'll look forward to being invited for a game and lunch. I hear nothing beats the roasted Romaine salad at the Lakeville Country Club." He patted Paul's back. "You're good to go."

Rolling his shoulders with relief, Paul laughed. "It may be a while. Autumn's sister arrives late tonight for two weeks, and…" He paused at the hand raised before him.

"I understand, Paul. Keep me in the loop and if there's anything we can do, don't hesitate to pick up that phone. The Merino family is here for your family. You make sure to get your own exercise time in. If you don't stay healthy, mentally and physically, you'll be no good to your wife." He cocked his eye at Paul.

"Promise." He threw a salute. "I'll see you next week, unless something comes up. I'll have Lucy confirm. Thanks." He refilled his pockets and threaded the belt back onto his waist. "See you in church?"

"Not this week. We have street ministry in Strattsburg this weekend. When Autumn is feeling better, you and the girls should join us." He opened the door and led Paul through the empty waiting room.

"I think when she is feeling better, she would love that. She misses going to the women's shelter. Life got too busy. It should never be 'too busy' to be about what God lays on your heart to do." They shook hands at the door. "Stay well."

"Godspeed," Dean replied. He prayed for the Pyoriasaari family as he watched Paul drive away from his office.

Bundled in a sweater, flannel pajama pants and a light fleece throw, despite the late June heatwave, Autumn sat on the couch listening to Jacquie's final practice session. One of the very few regrets of her childhood was the fact that she did not learn to play any instruments. Her stern grandmother offered to pay for lessons for all of her grandchildren, but Autumn's father would have none of her charity. One of the things Autumn insisted on and saved purposely for were music lessons. Emily hadn't shown interest thus far.

Her eyes filled with tears; Jacquie played beautifully. "I wish this blasted chemo could have waited till after the recital," she muttered, lost in the strains of *Summer*, one of Jacquie's favored selections. They'd had some strained discussions about Autumn missing the event.

Autumn noted the fervor with which Jacquie practiced the past few days. Both she and Paul assured the girls that the cancer was removed and the chemotherapy was a preventative measure. Emily reverted to pouty toddler-like attitudes when worried. Jacquie threw herself into music.

The back door slid open and Emily's squeal announced her father's arrival home. She heard him walk through to Jacquie and speak to her intently a few moments. Autumn smiled when he appeared with Emily perched on his back. He swung her around and placed her on a chair before taking a seat by Autumn.

"How are you?" he asked before brushing a kiss on her cheek. "Dean asked after you."

"You didn't tell him how I feel about his drink, did you?" She grimaced. "I don't know what he calls it."

"I did not tell him how vile you find it. I did show him your picture, though." She poked his ribs. "In my defense, he asked about it. He also invited us to join them for street ministry when you are feeling better." He laid an arm across the back of the couch.

She laid her head on his shoulder. "That would be a good thing to consider. We're so sheltered here." She snuggled more tightly against him. "Nothing terrible happens in Lakeville."

He hid an amused grin. "I'm sure your brother-in-law, the Lakeville detective, would disagree."

"Probably," she replied, fighting the fatigue that so suddenly overwhelmed her. "Please don't forget to video tonight. I'm so…" A large yawn interrupted.

He stood. "You need to rest. Come, now. I'll get you settled and the girls can come up and say goodbye before we go. You'll have plenty of video from all angles." He held his hands out.

When she lifted her hands to his, their eyes met. The depth of their love was communicated with the most subtle of movements. A nod, a turn of the corner of a mouth upwards, the lift of cheeks. Autumn was enveloped in it as Paul led her up the stairs to their room.

Silas stirred a large pan full of sausage as Emily watched, mesmerized by every move he made. Jacquie and Aina chatted about the recitals in the living room, flanked by Wynter, Sunnie and Storm attempting to catch up on family news. Jude and Tom had younger children of the male variety corralled in the back yard.

Paul prepared a large pot of coffee. The hum of Autumn's family was balm to his soul. He often wondered what it would be like to have a large family when he was a child. He experienced acceptance and warmth in the Young family. It was unlike the love he knew at home. Although he sensed that was changing.

"Can I stir now, Uncle Si?" Emily's tone was full of eagerness.

He handed her the spoon. "Remember, slowly and evenly. No grease will splash if you do it that way. What should we make with all of this?"

"I get to pick?" She almost dropped the wood spoon on the floor. She spun around on the step stool. "Did you hear that, Daddy? Uncle Si is going to let me pick what to make!"

"I bet I can tell him what you'll pick," Paul said. He pulled coffee mugs from the cabinet.

She turned back to Silas. "Is there enough to make gravy biscuits and scrambled sausage eggs?"

He stifled his chuckle over the deep intensity of her expression. "I'm sure there is, Emmie. That's almost 5 pounds of sausage. I want to be sure you have enough for breakfasts for a while."

"Mommy doesn't eat a lot," she informed him. "The chemo-cals make her not hungry." She resumed stirring. "We need cheese and eggs."

"Yes, ma'am." Silas nodded seriously before heading to the refrigerator for supplies. He paused by Paul.

"I put some other meals in the freezer. Jacquie knows what they are. If you need anything else, let us know." He pulled the door open and removed eggs. "Mom is cooking tonight, she said she'll bring it all over around four."

Paul reached past him to pluck a package of shredded cheese from a drawer. "Thank you. This is all very helpful. Julie has organized the women at church to come by, too. Sunnie insisted on sending over the women who clean her house." He handed the bag to Silas. "I don't mind admitting to you that the idea of someone I don't know cleaning my house doesn't sit well with me." Paul left them to their gourmet cooking lesson to go check on Autumn.

With a laugh, Silas started back to the stove. "Emmie, we need two bowls. One for the eggs and cheese and one for the extra sausage."

Jacquie threw an exasperated look at her aunts. Talk of the recital stirred up the discontent that she felt over her mother missing it. Aina had joined in the discussion, enjoying stories of Storm's British adventures.

She rose and wandered through the kitchen. Emily and Silas were elbow-deep in culinary creations. She continued out to the patio. Her cousins were leap-frogging while her uncles talked in the far corner of the yard. She sighed, walking along the edge of the concrete until she came to the block with the family handprints.

Jacquie squatted, pulling her skirt around her ankles. She remembered the day her father poured the blocks, her mother's very last task on his renovation honey-do list. It had to set for an hour before Paul allowed the girls to place their hands in the cool, wet sludge. The pattern of hands created a heart, and Autumn carefully inscribed the notation *Joshua 24:15.*

Jacquie recited part of the passage to herself. "As for me and my house, we will serve the Lord."

Her hand skimmed the surface, fingers tracing the impression of her mother's hand. Everywhere she looked in the yard, her mother was imprinted—the garden she loved, the plants on the patio she repotted. In the large painted quilt block that decorated the back of the house and the smaller ones hanging along the fence. It was Autumn who made their house their home. She created the loving environment in which Jacquie felt loved and secure.

"I hate cancer," she whispered. The sobs broke through the tightness in her throat, and she found herself collapsing into strong arms. Jacquie sensed the sudden quiet in the yard and someone herding the group of boys into the house. Her uncle—she wasn't certain which one—stayed with her. It was a relief to release the tears.

"I know it's not as pretty as Grammie's, but I promise it has no oil on it," Jude said to her, offering a deep blue bandana to soak up the tears. She sniffle-laughed and took it from his hand. He kept an arm around her shoulders as the emotions settled.

Jude pointed, drawing her attention upwards. Dabbing at her eyes, Jacquie looked to see a bank of clouds; large, fluffy clouds against the brilliant blue sky. They formed a strip of cotton-like flowers over Lakeville. The corners of her mouth began to turn.

"I knew a smile was hiding in there." Jude squeezed her shoulder. "Do you want a few minutes to yourself?"

"Okay," she initially agreed. Then, when he began to get up she changed her mind. "No. Would you stay here?"

He nodded and sat back down. He clasped his hands in front of his knees. They sat in silence, watching the clouds drift and eventually break up. Jacquie wiped her nose on the cloth, then looked aghast.

"Oh, Uncle Jude, I'm sorry! I'll wash it for you!"

He threw his head back and laughed. "It's fine. That's what they're for. It's better than anything I wipe on it at the shop." He placed a hand on her shoulder. "I know what it feels like to be afraid someone you love might die. It's not a good feeling."

Remembering when her cousin was born and that both he and her aunt had been close to death sobered Jacquie. Uncle Jude stayed by their sides for days before Julie began to show signs of improvement.

"Your mom is going to be fine," he assured her, and she knew he was speaking a truth. "But, any time you're scared and feel like crying, you call me. I'll come right over."

For the first time in her life, Jacquie saw the resemblance between her mother and brother. It was the smile. It lit their faces and touched the depths of the recipient's heart.

"I will, Uncle Jude. I think…" She paused, inhaled deeply and exhaled, feeling cleansed. "I think I might want to be alone for a minute." She returned her uncle's smile with a wobbly one of her own.

"Sure. Just don't forget," he pointed at her. "I'm only a phone call away. Any of us are." He winked, leaning in to place a kiss on her forehead before he left her alone.

After a few moments of contemplation and another glance at the handprints, Jacquie folded her hands and placed them in her lap. Her head bowed, a new level in maturity of her faith began to form as she unburdened her heart about this situation that no one asked for, but the family had been thrust into.

Chapter 14

Hearing the rumble of familiar voices in the kitchen, Autumn attempted to force herself out of grogginess. The sound of deep laughter drifting into the bedroom window jogged her to rouse more. *Sounds like Daddy*, she thought. *I must be dreaming again.* She'd been plagued by odd images during the first few nights after the treatments. She rolled over, stretched and finger-combed through her hair.

Paul opened the door as a startled cry erupted. Autumn sat up in their bed, staring forlornly at a hand full of silky, deep brown hair. She began to reach her other hand to take stock of what remained.

"Belle, stop." He shut the door and hurried to her side. She fell against him, weeping. He held her close, waiting out the current emotional storm.

"I'm sorry," she said when the shock wore off. "It's amazing how one pill a week can turn your life upside down. I knew it would happen, but I didn't expect to wake up to it." She looked down again at the clump in her hand and the pillow covered with locks. "I guess I should brush it out and see how much is still attached." A sigh escaped.

"Let me help." He rose, retrieved her brush and sat back down. Gently he stroked through Autumn's formerly lustrous hair. It detached from her scalp with alarming ease and the job was over quickly. "Do you want to look?"

She nodded, then shook her head, going through the same motions several times. "Oh, this is silly! Of course I want to look." She gingerly touched what little remained. "At least there's some left."

"It's probably prudent to shave the rest. You've been anxious to experiment with the scarves your mother brought when she stopped over last week." Several times he found her watching tutorials online of elaborate dome dècor. To his relief, she laughed.

"I do! Okay...I'm ready. Come with me." She held out her hand.

"Belle...there's something I should tell you before we go..." Before he could say more, she heard another deep laugh that she was certain she dreamed. Confusion reigned a short moment, then recognition dawned.

"Of course. Jude is here? I thought...oh, it was weird, Paul! I thought I dreamed about my father again." She walked to the window and looked into the yard.

"Is that Tom?" She looked closer, although her sister Sunnie's brawny, red-headed husband couldn't be mistaken. "Who else is here?"

"We wanted to surprise you," he began. "Jude picked her up last night..."

She spun away from the window. "*Her?* Is Storm here? I told her not to...oh, but I am so glad she ignored me!"

Delighted the news wasn't devastating considering the state of her appearance, he watched her bustle around the room. An infusion of new energy seemed to drive her. Autumn picked out an outfit, matching it with one of the new accessories provided by Sammie.

"I think I can knot this to the side." She lifted the scarf, examining it and pondering the potential. "It may not be perfect, but I'll get better." She lowered it and smiled at him. "I'm ready," she said. "Take me to see what's left of my hair before you shave it all off."

The image of his wife, smiling despite the trial she was walking through, was forever locked in the annals of his mind. Before lathering Autumn's head with shaving cream they snapped pictures, both silly and poignant, that they would share with the girls at a later point in time.

When Paul returned to the gathering, he pulled Jacquie and Emily aside. His attempted cloak of privacy was shattered by Emily's gasp as he shared the news of Autumn's new appearance. The family discussions ceased in time for Sammie's arrival and request for help carrying hot dinner items, which was a perfect diversion for Emily's attention.

As others rallied to either carry hot casserole dishes or start setting up the assembly line of plates and utensils, Jacquie quietly headed up the stairs. She lightly knocked on her parent's bedroom door.

"Come," Autumn called. When Jacquie opened the door, Autumn was standing at the dresser, scarf in hand and a look of profound concentration visible. The completion the creation ended when the green silk cloth slid from her fingers—the scarf slumped around her head. She turned from the reflection, and her frustrated expression gave way to a fit of giggles. Jacquie rushed over and lifted the shroud of emerald. They hugged, laughing together.

"Maybe this one is too slippery to start with," she said. "Which knot were you trying?"

"This one," Autumn showed her the video playing on a tablet device. The style was referred to as a twisted crown. They watched it through twice, then, with Jacquie's help, Autumn accomplished a reasonable replication.

"Well, I can see you'll be helping me more often than I thought," Autumn said, patting the entwined creation with satisfaction.

"I'd love to, Mom." She looked in the mirror at their reflection. "You look beautiful."

"Good enough for everyone, including Aunt Storm?" Autumn laughed again, this time at Jacquie's surprise. "Dad told me before. They aren't exactly a quiet group. I thought I heard Grammie, too. Did she make Thanksgiving dinner?"

"No, it smelled like Italian. Probably lasagna, and it looked like more than dinner for tonight. Uncle Si and Emmie were making breakfast casseroles while you were sleeping. Aunt Storm, Aunt Julie and Aunt Sunnie have been talking in the living room."

Her description of the morning's activities ended abruptly. Sensing information of a more private nature about to unload, Autumn glanced at her daughter, then picked up a make-up brush and a compact. "I think I'll put a little color on my face…"

"I went outside and started to cry." Jacquie looked down, fingering a necklace lying on the dresser. "I was looking at our handprints. I got so mad, then scared. I hate that you're sick!" She sniffed.

Putting down the cosmetics, Autumn pulled Jacquie into an embrace. "It's okay, sweetie." She amused herself privately at her use of her own mother's favored endearment. "I get angry and scared too. That's when I start to pray harder."

"That's what Uncle Jude said. He said that I can always call him. That was nice."

"My brother is a nice guy," Autumn agreed, releasing her. She resumed swishing the brush across her cheekbone. "He means it, too. He'll drop everything to be here for you. All of them would. I'm—we're--very blessed to have such a wonderful family." She made one final swipe. "There. How's that?" She turned to Jacquie.

"Perfect." Jacquie smiled. "Like you always do. I love you, Mom."

The hug that followed was tear-filled.

Glancing at the clock in the living room for one last time, Storm stood up. "This is silly, I am going to get her." She left the room, carefully stepping over nieces and nephews playing a board game on the floor.

Storm's announcement spurred others to make the feast ready to consume. A flurry of activity began. At Paul's suggestion of *al fresco* dining, the men carried chairs outside while women brought trays being kept warm in the oven out to the table. Silas, taking charge of the kitchen, as always, had begun pouring tomato sauce into a serving bowl. Tom joined him, and was unsuccessfully conducting a search for a bread knife.

"I think it's over there, dude." Silas nodded in the direction of drawers he thought most likely to house sharp utensils. Sunnie breezed into the room, walked directly to a previously searched area and produced the desired object. She smiled to Tom, then walked back out to the table on the patio.

"Sometimes I think she should be wearing the badge," Tom muttered before following behind. Keeping his amusement well hidden, Silas finished his task, picked up a ladle and joined the family in waiting on Autumn's grand entrance.

The sisters met on the stairs in a flurry of greetings and hugs. Jacquie slid past them to allow the tearful reunion. It lasted only a few moments, then Storm pulled back and looked at Autumn, mentally assessing every detail of her appearance.

"You look fabulous! How long has it been since you lost hair, you didn't tell me that last time we spoke! Is that one of the scarves Mom got for you?"

"Thanks, just this morning, and yes." Autumn gave quick responses to the questions Storm peppered her with. "You should talk about not telling about things! I told you not to come. When did you plan this?"

They found their way to the kitchen as the conversation continued. Autumn pulled two large glasses from a cabinet and then went to the fridge.

"Since you had the surgery," Storm confessed, accepting a glass filled with ice. "I arranged emergency financing with Mom and Vic. Of course, I had to promise to come back with the kids for Christmas." She rolled her eyes. "The things I do for you!"

"Well, I appreciate it. I know funds are tight, I didn't want you to feel obligated…" She paused and poured lemonade into their glasses. "Since you did come, you get to take me to Vic's cancer group get-together this weekend." She lifted her glass. "I'm glad you're here."

They toasted each other. They could hear the family outside; welcoming sounds of conversation and laughter. Storm took the glass from Autumn's hand, placed it on the counter next to hers and linked arms with her.

"Let's go," she said, pulling Autumn with her as she often did when they were small. The crowd outside cheered her appearance, then linked hands around her to pray over the provision of family, food and restoration of health.

Chapter 15

Victoria's quarter mile driveway was awash in soft lighting. Pink and white ribbon bedecked every tree along the way. The magnificent farm house glowed faint pink, signature ribbons adorning each column of the wrap around porch.

"I think I'm getting tired of pink," Autumn commented as Storm pulled the van around the drive to the front of the steps. "It's never been my favorite color."

"I remember, you always preferred blue. You'll grow to love it, I'm sure. Tolerate it, at least." Storm shut the engine and looked closely at her sister. "Are you up for this?" The past week had been busy...Storm could see the shadows under Autumn's eyes.

"I'll be fine. You'll be here, even if it's upstairs on Skype with your husband. I'm resigned to obedience—no overdoing. I do wish this was a dinner for couples," she admitted before they exited the van. "I so much wanted Paul to hear some of their stories."

A minor squabble erupted when Storm insisted on linking arms on the way to the door. As they lighted the porch steps, she chided Autumn, "If you drop any more weight, you'll be as skinny as Sunnie."

"Paul is somewhat aghast over that fact," Autumn said. "It's been hard to keep anything down even with taking the Zofran. The concoction he got from Dean isn't helping as much as he hoped. Other times I am just not hungry. I keep telling him, it's just a season. The bright side of losing weight is that Sunnie has a few beautiful outfits that I can now borrow."

They were still giggling as they arrived at the door. Victoria swept it open, a welcoming smile on her face. "Autumn! I am so happy that you made it." She was immediately enveloped in a swirl of *Chanel No 5* and the lacy scarf Victoria had wrapped around her shoulders.

Leaning past Autumn, Victoria brushed Storm's cheek with a kiss. "How are you, dear? I spoke to Steven this morning, the children are keeping him quite busy. It's good for him," she stated. A large wink punctuated her amusement over her son's parenting situation and affection for her daughter-in-law. She led them into the kitchen to join the gathering.

Women mingled around a punch bowl on one side of the kitchen. Others walked towards the living room, laughing together over a private joke. The story of the disease that bound them together was told in varying stages of hair loss and head coverings. One woman stood alone, eyeing the others with a mixture of curiosity and distrust.

An array of Depression glass dishes, cups, plates lined the marble topped island in varying shades of Autumn's recently chosen "most likely to become loathed" color. She threw a parting eye roll in her sister's direction and proceeded to the punch bowl. Storm wandered upstairs to call her family.

The group reminisced over a former member before sharing stories of struggles and successes. Autumn was warmly welcomed into their exclusive club. The lone woman Autumn noticed when she arrived was also new and only smiled tightly when introduced. Victoria shared some encouraging thoughts before praying a blessing over the food.

At the island, Autumn picked up a festive plate before walking through the buffet line. She dished up a few pickled eggs of a shocking pink hue, a small portion of salmon topped with a balsamic glaze, a serving of strawberry topped salad, and quinoa pilaf that was—thankfully—nutty brown in color.

She sought out the wicker chaise in the three season porch. . Her head was spinning from her recently returned appetite. She smiled to others as she crossed to the north corner of the room. Autumn situated herself, looking forward to digging into her meal.

Another woman entered. They nodded to each other before she sat across the room—it was the woman who didn't seem comfortable being there. She took a seat on an overstuffed wicker chair and placed her plate on her lap.

"You're Victoria's daughter-in-law?" The gruff question surprised Autumn.

"Oh, no, that was…is…my sister, Storm. I'm Autumn Pyoriasaari. My…our mother and Victoria are very good friends." She smiled, hoping to engage her in a friendly exchange.

"My name is Angie. Angie Bates. I'm on week 5 of 10 of my chemo. Had a double a month ago…I…well, I met Victoria…"

Angie stopped and looked from left to right, as though searching for something. Confusion, fright and then resignation flew across her face.

"This has got to stop!" She placed the plate on a low table beside the chair. "I hate these mood swings. I am not a forgetful person! I want my life back to normal. Now!" Angie hung her head in her hands and cried.

Tears of solidarity swiftly welled for Autumn over Angie's plight. Abandoning her dinner, she went to offer comfort. She prayed aloud over Angie for strength, as she had so many times for herself. She prayed for release from weariness and exhaustion. She interceded with pleas for patience with the endless cycle of treatments.

Others gathered around, placing hands on Angie's head or shoulders, offering their brand of support. When her sobbing subsided, Angie shrugged off the consolation and wiped her eyes on the back of her knobby hand. The small crowd dispersed.

Autumn returned to the chaise. She poked at the salad, nibbled a strawberry; hunger had fled again. Autumn put the plate down, sat back and closed her eyes, thinking back over the impromptu prayer meeting. A smile emerged. Unaware that Angie watched her, Autumn raised one hand and silently praised God for the opportunity He had presented.

She started when Angie bluntly declared, "I dunno how you have such peace. I'm so tired. Tired of inconveniencing family, friends, and my husband. I'd like nothing better than to hurl this dish across the porch and watch shattered glass fall on the floor. Aren't you angry?"

Autumn turned to face her. "I could be. At times I am, but only for a moment. I remember that we are not promised anything but His peace when we seek Him. We're not guaranteed health, riches, or a grand home. I trust that whatever it is that I find myself going through, it's because He allowed it."

"You'll excuse me, but, that's a load of bunk." Angie violently poked her fork into a morsel on her plate. "Being angry is part of the process. If you want to lie to yourself and think there's some cosmic reason behind everything, well, you go right ahead."

An unsettling silence fell on the room. Angie concentrated on finishing her meal, ignoring all who came alongside her only moments before. When she rose, she walked away without a look back. Autumn picked up her plate, intent on following Angie.

She entered the kitchen as Angie slammed out of the house. The sound of an engine revving signaled her departure. Autumn walked to the sink and began running hot water, an air of defeat settling around her. She added a liberal squirt of dish soap and watched the tub fill with bubbles.

Storm walked down the large staircase and headed for the porch, knowing her sister enjoyed that particular spot in the house. She was surprised to find Autumn washing dishes as tears silently rolled down her cheeks.

She stepped up next to her and pulled the sponge from Autumn's hand. "What's wrong? Why are you washing dishes when there's a dishwasher right next to you?"

Autumn snatched the sponge back and began vigorously scrubbing the counter. "Just leave me alone. I need a little..."

"You do not need to exhaust yourself. Give me that, now!" They wrestled over the dripping yellow object a moment, then Autumn gave in. Storm tossed it in the sink, grabbed Autumn's hand and led her to a small office.

"In all the years I've been here in this house, I've never been in George's office," Autumn said.

"It's the only place I can think of where no one will interrupt us. Now, tell me, what in the world is bothering you?"

Flopping into a stylish leather chair by the desk, Autumn began to recall the events of the evening. When she reached the part where Angie stormed out, the tears flowed again.

"I've had opportunities to talk to other women about how faith is carrying me through this. I don't think it's impacted a single one. Why go through all of this—the surgery, the chemo, losing my hair—if I can't even adequately explain why I'm going through this?"

Storm sat on the floor cross-legged. "Steve and I been in ministry a long time. One thing we discovered early on is that we may never see results of laboring for the faith." She leaned back a moment before going on. "You did what your faith required of you. You told others how you are making it through this. That's where your responsibility ends, Autumn. It's the same as Paul told the Corinthian church 2000 years ago: someone waters, someone plants a seed, but it's God who grants the increase."

Autumn fiddled with the fringe on her scarf. "I'm not sure I like your answer. I'm not sure why I'm not sure, but I'm not sure." She scowled when Storm tossed her head back and laughed.

"That's pride talking. You need to get over that, and fast." She stood and walked over to Autumn. "The reason you don't recognize it is because it's something that you rarely struggle with. Unless I try to help you up or walk or something else along those lines." She offered her hand.

She smiled and took her sister's hand. "It's good to have you in my life." She stood with Storm's help and then wrapped her arms around her. "Even when I don't enjoy what you say." It was a lesson Autumn would not forget.

Epilogue

Cool weather descended on Lakeville during October, in time for Autumn's post-chemotherapy PET scan. The family looked forward to a visit with Paul's parents as the procedure was scheduled with Dr. Mahr in Philadelphia.

A long stretch of highway allowed Autumn to contemplate the summer months; customarily they were filled with long, lazy afternoons, family picnics and nights on the patio under the stars. This year had been vastly different. Their family matured in significant ways. Their marriage was invigorated by walking through tough times together, and served to intensify their appreciation of each other. She was grateful that they faithfully weathered the storm.

Emily and Jacquie played a game in the back seat of the van. Autumn smiled, listening to their banter and laughter. They were one of the many the joys of her life. Emily was becoming a little lady, and Jacquie, a fine mentor and role model for her younger sister.

Spirits were high; everyone was expecting and praying for a good report. "I feel very good about this, Paul," Autumn said.

"As do I, belle." He glanced in the rear view mirror, preparing to change lanes. "You went through the chemo well. I know it didn't feel like it to you, but you did."

Paul's words resonated within her. She had come through physically and spiritually stronger. "Thanks be to God," she said, the catch in her throat welcome and expected. It meant she was alive, felt deeply and experienced fully what the Lord put before her.

"Paul, sit down!" Astrid turned from the dressing table mirror to her husband. Every sound outside the townhouse caused him to rocket from the settee to the window. "Honestly, you'd think Paul and his family had never been to visit us before."

He paced back to the chair, wiping imagined particles from the jacquard fabric before he returned to his seat. Taking up the magazine he discarded a moment before, he flipped back to the article that caught his fancy.

"Did you know, my dear, that studies have shown a marked improvement in patients going through chemotherapy using certain herbal concoctions? In the UK they've been treating with a mix of traditional and herbal protocols for years. They are, by far, more open-minded than we are in the U.S."

Hiding the grin that was spreading, Astrid picked up a tail comb and teased some of her fringe into place. This side of her husband, one she knew and fell in love with years before, was as fresh and exciting as the first time he smiled at her. Instead of bemoaning the years he'd buried himself in grief and denial, she rejoiced in the small daily discoveries.

At the sound of car doors and Emily's laughter, Paul Sr. closed the magazine and hurried from the bedroom. Astrid returned the comb to the vanity, made a final check of her appearance and left the room, as anxious as her husband was to see the family.

"Your hair is adorable! Will you keep it short for a little while?" Astrid placed a tall glass of iced tea in front of Autumn and leaned on the counter.

"I'm not sure. It's certainly different than what I'm used to." Autumn patted the new, soft locks forming loose waves around her face. "The last time my hair was this short, I was barely old enough to remember! My mom gave me a few old pictures." She produced them from her pocketbook. "Emmie thinks she looks just like me."

As Astrid thumbed through the photographs, an indulgent grin, the unmistakable mark of a proud grandmother, grew. "She is right, dear. Goodness, but she does look just like you! Which sister is which?"

Autumn looked at the shot Astrid held out. "That's Storm," she pointed to the young girl on one side of the snapshot. "And, that's Sunnie." She pointed to the other. "I think this may have been the only year we wore matching Christmas dresses."

Astrid set the photos aside and took Autumn's hands. "Tell me...are you nervous?"

Without the slightest hesitation, Autumn answered. "No." She smiled. "Not at all. This experience has taught me so much. I cherish Paul more than ever. I'm so thankful for my girls. My family—in Lakeville and Philadelphia—has stood by me and loved me." The women hugged. "I am ready for whatever God has in store for me." Autumn picked up a napkin and dabbed her eyes.

"I think my husband is nervous," Astrid said, stepping to the sink. She, too, dabbed at her eyes with a stray bit of paper towel. "But, he has been praying. It has been beautiful to hear. He is looking forward to Sunday. He wants to share worship time with his son." She paused. Her voice trembled as she concluded. "He says that it is something he regrets missing when Paul was growing up."

Humbled by her mother-in-law's implicit trust, Autumn rose and went to her. Their embrace expressed the newly discovered depth emerging in the relationship. Beauty was being formed from ashes, as promised.

"Incredible," Dr. Mahr repeated with each step she took on her way to Paul Sr.'s office. The results of Autumn's test in hand, her feet followed the familiar path through the hospital. She was so intent on her thoughts concerning the results, she barreled past Paul Sr. in the hallway. She spun when he called out to her.

"Where are you off to, and looking so serious?"

"To see you," she admitted. She walked towards him, waving the paperwork in her hand. "I have Autumn's results."

"Very good!" He started to his office when she joined him. "I've been waiting for good news." He guffawed at the bewildered look she tossed his way.

Convention was set aside the moment they were inside his door. "Paul, this is, well...amazing is my only adjective," she announced. "I've seen many women who we've pronounced cancer-free, but never this soon after surgery and chemotherapy."

When he held out his hand for the report, she noticed they trembled. Witnessing the stoic surgeon unabashedly shed tears topped her astonishment of the report. When he sat at his desk, folded his hands and began to pray, she stood by in awkward silence. He completed his communing by raising his hands and shouting "Hallelujah!" which caused several people walking past to poke their heads in the door.

"I think you need a psych eval, Paul," Dr. Mahr suggested before motioning for the spectators to be on their way.

"Why, Gen? This is an amazing miracle, and I'm happy to tell anyone who asks." He reread the report. "Have you called them yet?"

"I wanted to give you the option," she said.

He got up, looking out of the window a moment before crossing the room. He placed the report in her hands. "You are kind to consider me a part of this, Gen. It's your news to share. I thank you for letting me know."

Meaning to only thank him and leave, the words that poured from Dr. Mahr were jumbled; hurried. They would not be stopped. "I don't understand this, Paul, nor can I comprehend this change that has come over you. It's not obvious, yet it is. You are the same, yet remarkably changed."

A gentle smile, one that radiated contentment, touched her more than the previous tears. "I thank Jesus that you noticed. Go on, call Autumn. I'm sure they'll enjoy hearing from you."

He ushered her out and shut the office door softly before walking to the newest appliance in the room. After admiring it a moment, he reached in the burnished aluminum mini-fridge and pulled a bottle of carrot juice from it. The former furnishings and its contents had been removed, replaced with items which encouraged and supported emotional and physical well-being.

Paul Sr. carried the bottle to his desk. He gazed at the pictures clustered in the right quadrant; Emily and Jacquie, he and Astrid, Paul and Autumn. When he sat, he took a frame from the left. The quality of the picture inside wasn't as sharp as the others. It showed wear and age. Paul Sr. loved everything about it.

"We made it," he said. "Autumn is cancer free. An amazing miracle. A chance you should have had, dear sister." He sipped from the bottle. "She's so much like you—like I imagine you would have been, had you survived."

When memories began to emerge, he welcomed them. No longer did he dread thinking about Karin; he welcomed the opportunity to celebrate her life. He looked from the picture to the legal pad on his desk. Line upon line of remembrances were written, which blossomed into the foundation for one way in which he could—and would—honor her legacy.

He checked his watch. "Gen should be conferring with them now. I will feign surprise when they call me. I promise." He winked at the photo. "*Angel's Song* will help many, Karin. It will give them hope and the means to access the care that wasn't available to you. So much has changed."

Karin seemed to be in agreement with her brother. He stroked the glass preserving the photo. "I hope that Paul will consider coming alongside of me in this. You can learn much once your heart has been touched. Yes," he softly spoke, as though her essence would evaporate with volume. "Perhaps, one day, we may find a cure."

Paul joined Autumn on the patio once Emily was read to and prayed with. He unfurled a delightfully patterned throw. He fussed with it a moment, making sure it was carefully tucked around Autumn before he sat back. The chimenea's orange glow and the scent of freshly lit fireplaces surrounded them.

"It took Emmie three...no, four story books to finally settle in," Paul said, fatherly amusement painting his tone. "Her prayers were full of thanksgiving."

"Jacquie's were too," she agreed. "They were so happy at dinner tonight. I felt a bit funny calling Storm in the middle of her night, but she was forgiving when she heard the news." She giggled thinking of the call. Storm had gone from sleepy to animated in less than 0.8 seconds.

Paul worked his arm around her shoulders. "I'm happy to be the cause of rejoicing for the family on this night." He looked up at the stars over Lakeville as he continued his thoughts. "In May, I was afraid that we'd never enjoy another night like this. That our lives were going to change, and not in the way they have. This is not something I would ever have chosen for us. I can honestly say that I am grateful for walking through it."

He pulled her close and kissed her temple. She leaned into him and laid her arm across his chest. They spent a long evening in the chaise enjoying the crisp evening air until quiet affirmations of their devotion moved their celebration indoors.

Lying next to Paul as he slept later in the night, blissful tears flowed for Autumn. Reflecting on their conversation as she listened to his steady breathing, she agreed with his earlier assessment. She would not have chosen the path their lives followed the past months, but the lessons learned were eternal. Honoring the Teacher of those lessons would be a life's journey, and one well spent. Rolling to one side, she yawned and began to hum, anticipating the gift of sleep to blanket her.

Take my life, and let it be consecrated, Lord, to Thee. Take my moments and my days; let them flow in ceaseless praise.

Acknowledgements

This project has been a long time in process, from the very first inkling from the Lord that I should write it and why I should, to its completion.

My first and foremost thanks go to Him; He gifted me with the creativity to witness His truths in this manner. I humbly submit this finished work for His honor and glory.

My dear friend Karen Levine ~ it's such a joy to know you and minister with you. You are a shining example of living your convictions when it may not be easy to do so. Keep on keepin' on, sister!

Many thanks to Krista Mize who came alongside me when I needed a good and gracious person to edit this project. Krista, your encouragement, support and excitement as you got to know characters that have been beloved to me for many years was inspiring. Thank you for being a champion of Lakeville.

To the many who prayed for this project; my sisters in Community Bible Study and online friends across the globe. I appreciate your support and encouragement.

As always, thank you to my husband and friend who sacrifices hours as I type, have melt downs over formatting, complain about the cover creating software and so much more. You are the best thing in my life. Thank you for allowing me to pursue this crazy dream of becoming a writer.

Made in the USA
San Bernardino, CA
07 September 2015